22.76

What readers say about *What If the Queen Should Die?*

'An antidote to the Tudor domination of recent years' –
Annabel Gaskell

'JP Flintoff brings to light the life and troubled times of Queen Anne, and he does so with considerable grace and aplomb' –
Rachel Stirling

'The book gets better and better as it proceeds, becoming very tense and gripping at the finale' – Simon Kingston

'Fast paced, hilarious and unexpected . . . Should be made into a play, or TV mini-series' – Ella Jakobson

'Loved it! The drama, the pace, the intrigue, the comedy, the weaving together of history and plausible invention' –
Philip Stewart

'The descriptions of eighteenth-century life will be with me for years. It had never occurred to me that losing a king or queen could be like losing a parent . . . Fantastic' – Kylie Rixon

'I found the book intriguing, joyously difficult to put down. It kept calling me back from whatever I was doing, urging me to read on. The form feels anarchic yet sumptuous. A feast for readers who enjoy their books stylishly written and cleverly plotted' –
Victoria Lambert

'Queen Anne cuts at times a pathetic figure, at the mercy of those around her, but also touched by deep tragedy – and when the time comes, shows her strength' –   Claire Murray

'It brings the characters of the great writers – Swift, Pope and Defoe – to life' –   Hazel Stevens

'Defoe progresses from a man looking to redeem himself in the eyes of his family and society to a man who changes the course of history' –   Jenny O'Gorman

'Memorably vivid, a flair for dialogue, exceptional talent' –
                                                          Ita Marquess

'I loved the book. Really thrilling. Truly wonderful' – Mark Vent

'Brilliant and amusing' –   Camille Sharma

'I loved the information at the end, as to how he completed the book, using improvisation and crowd-funding. Great to show the struggle – as all good stories do' –   Lizzie Palmer

'Quirky, unique . . . a book that is really about the art of story-telling. It has left me bedazzled' –   Una Lynch

John-Paul Flintoff is an award-winning writer and performer. His books have been published in 14 languages. He has worked as a bin man, executive PA, scuba diver, poet, taxi driver, tailor, gardener, ice-cream salesman, film-maker, assistant undertaker, ceramics designer, bit-part player in pantomime, waiter, illustrator, high-wire window cleaner, painter and decorator, karaoke singer, rat catcher and executive coach. But writing comes first.

By John-Paul Flintoff:

Comp: A Survivor's Tale
Sew Your Own
How To Change The World
The Family Project (with Harriet Green)

WHAT IF
THE QUEEN
SHOULD DIE?

by

John-Paul Flintoff

unbound

unbound

This edition first published in 2016

Unbound
6th Floor Mutual House 70 Conduit Street London W1S 2GF
www.unbound.co.uk

© John-Paul Flintoff, 2016

The right of John-Paul Flintoff to be identified as the author of this work
has been asserted in accordance with Section 77 of the Copyright,
Designs and Patents Act 1988. No part of this publication may be copied,
reproduced, stored in a retrieval system, or transmitted, in any form
or by any means without the prior permission of the publisher, nor be
otherwise circulated in any form of binding or cover other than that in
which it is published and without a similar condition being imposed
on the subsequent purchaser.

While every effort has been made to trace the owners of copyright
material reproduced herein, the publisher would like to apologise for any
omissions and will be pleased to incorporate missing acknowledgments in
any further editions.

Text Design by Ellipsis Digital Limited, Glasgow

A CIP record for this book is available from the British Library

ISBN 978-1-78352-258-3 (trade hbk)
ISBN 978-1-78352-259-0 (ebook)
ISBN 978-1-78352-259-0 (limited edition)

Printed in Great Britain by Clays Ltd, St Ives Plc

1 3 5 7 9 8 6 4 2

Praise for John-Paul Flintoff's writing:

'Very good. Very funny . . . In fact, it made me laugh' –
Harold Pinter

Praise for *Comp*:
'Makes *The Lord of the Flies* look like a soft-soap cover-up' –
Guardian

'Very readable' –
Spectator

'Often funny in the blackest way imaginable' –
Times Educational Supplement

'Fun and honest' –
Literary Review

'Both supremely entertaining and an invaluable social document' –
Daily Telegraph

'Entertaining and thoughtful' – *Financial Times*

'Faint echoes of *Catcher in the Rye* and a nod to the wicked young [Martin] Amis, but mostly Flintoff writes as his own likeable, transparent self' –
New Statesman

Praise for *Sew Your Own*:
'Very honest and human and moving' –
Nick Rosen

'Wonderful, amazing, funny and warm' –
Tom Hodgkinson

For Catherine Thanki

Uphill!
(To M.B.)

What, and how great, the virtue and the art
That's manifested by my old friend Mart.
A student, once, in sleep, you cried, 'Uphill!'
Today you stand in pedals by me still:
Your own pledge made, you deftly fetched another
From Uncle Stephen first, and then your mother.
What moved them, by their pledge, to be so kind,
What words you used – in this I'm deaf, and blind.
Whatever! The point is, by expanding
My small crowd, you helped me get the funding.
Now Baxter is a factor, and you, Brookes,
Do make it possible to print my books.

Mapologists
(To T.B. and M.A.)

At Tina's flat now let us pass one day,
And see what might emerge from hours of play.
With ease, like Tina scootering through traffic,
We'll take an abstract concept, make it graphic.
Mike finds a strategy, ruse, tactic – all
To make the thing we build more practical.
Mapologists, your colourful displays
Make plain the hidden path through any maze:
Like, overcome What's Bugging You. Find presents.
Choose pets: cat, cockerpoo, mouse, snail or pheasant?
Collaborators, when I asked aloud
You read my thoughts on funding by the crowd,
Helped shape a plan, encouraged: 'Try Unbound!'
I then was lost, map-makers. Now I'm found.

Dear Reader,

The book you are holding came about in a rather different way to most others. It was funded directly by readers through a new website: Unbound. Unbound is the creation of three writers. We started the company because we believed there had to be a better deal for both writers and readers. On the Unbound website, authors share the ideas for the books they want to write directly with readers. If enough of you support the book by pledging for it in advance, we produce a beautifully bound special subscribers' edition and distribute a regular edition and e-book wherever books are sold, in shops and online.

This new way of publishing is actually a very old idea (Samuel Johnson funded his dictionary this way). We're just using the internet to build each writer a network of patrons. Here, at the back of this book, you'll find the names of all the people who made it happen.

Publishing in this way means readers are no longer just passive consumers of the books they buy, and authors are free to write the books they really want. They get a much fairer return too – half the profits their books generate, rather than a tiny percentage of the cover price.

If you're not yet a subscriber, we hope that you'll want to join our publishing revolution and have your name listed in one of our books in the future. To get you started, here is a £5 discount on your first pledge. Just visit unbound.com, make your pledge and type **thequeen** in the promo code box when you check out.

Thank you for your support,

Dan, Justin and John
Founders, Unbound

Contents

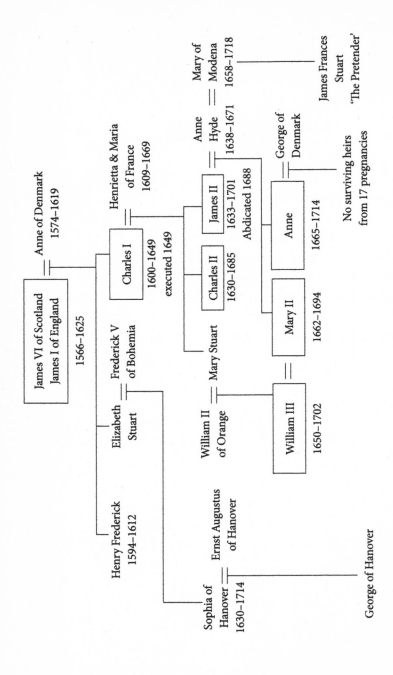

Foreword

Professor John Mullan, UCL

This period should interest anybody who's interested in literature, because many of the genres we enjoy today were either invented then, or transformed. It's a time of incredible invention in writing. The invention of journalism. Pope composed the most gorgeous, intricate satirical poetry ever written. Swift wrote the most deadly, frightening satirical prose. Daniel Defoe invented the novel.

The eighteenth century was an age of unparalleled irreverence and wit. The first book that really did it for me was something written later than Pope and Swift but very much influenced by them: *Tristram Shandy* was as weird and funny and clever as anything that anybody wrote in the twentieth century. It completely cured me of the inclination to condescend to the past – as if people in the past were 'like us but knew less'. No, no! In the eighteenth century they were cleverer than us, funnier than us, more brilliant than us. They used words better than us.

I wouldn't want to live then – too smelly, no analgesics – but their literature is better than anything we can imagine.

Who's Who

(main characters)

QUEEN ANNE. Protestant daughter of the late Catholic King James II, whom she helped to depose and exiled, along with her baby brother. James cursed Anne, and afterwards all of her children died before her. As she prepares for her own death, she must decide whether to make up for past wrongs and acknowledge her younger brother at last.

ABIGAIL, LADY MASHAM. Senior lady-in-waiting, thirty-five. Lady Masham knows she will not keep her prominence after the Queen dies, regardless of who inherits the crown. So Lady Masham steals from her mistress. A cousin of Oxford, whom she hates, and mistress of the much younger Bolingbroke.

LADY MARY ARDEN. Younger lady-in-waiting, aged seventeen. Overlooked by her seniors, Lady Mary hears and sees more than people realise. Her father is a Catholic who converted, reluctantly, to get ahead. Her sweetheart, Samuel Holland, is from a Protestant family that helped to remove King James.

DANIEL DEFOE. Failed businessman and occasional pamphleteer, mid-fifties. Has worked for years as a spy for the Earl of Oxford (even his wife has no idea about his secret life).

EARL OF OXFORD. The Queen's chief minister, mid-fifties, a Whig minister in coalition with Tory Bolingbroke (whom he hates). A personal friend to literary talents Jonathan Swift and Alexander Pope.

VISCOUNT BOLINGBROKE. Mid-thirties. Once Oxford's close friend but now a bitter rival. A great mind. Also a philanderer: Lady Masham is his mistress.

JAMES STUART, THE PRETENDER. Queen Anne's half-brother. Mid-twenties. Only son of Catholic James II. The Pretender was taken to France as a baby when his father was deposed.

JONATHAN SWIFT. Church of England priest, mid-forties. Writes propaganda for Oxford. Dreads being sent home to Ireland – the back of beyond.

ALEXANDER POPE. Fashionable, successful poet, mid-twenties. Severely affected by ill health: abdominal pain, inflamed eyes, stunted growth. As a Catholic, Pope is excluded from many careers and not allowed to live within ten miles of London.

SAMUEL HOLLAND. Lady Mary's sweetheart, aged eighteen. From a prominent Protestant family who helped to depose King James. He knows Mary's father will not want him as son-in-law.

WHAT IF
THE QUEEN
SHOULD DIE?

Chapter 1

The Adventure Begins

Daniel Defoe had been lying in bed, counting the minutes in his head until his wife's breathing had told him she was sleeping. And then he must have fallen asleep. What time was it? He had to be ready, and leave before daybreak. Even now, to do what he needed to do, it might be too late.

He could only guess at the hour because there was no light in the room, and he'd recently had to sell off his pocket-watch. He reckoned it must be almost three in the morning.

He hadn't imagined it would be possible to fall asleep tonight, because he'd gone to bed so disturbed. Shortly after sunset, he'd sensed the presence of a stranger outside the house, and gone outside with a candle.

'Who's there?' he asked, looking towards the great elm.

A tall man stepped towards him.

'We have found you, sir.'

'Who are you?'

'I know you, sir.'

The man's accent was from the north somewhere. But not far north. Stoke? Derby?

'What do you know of me?' asked Defoe.

'I know you owe a thousand pounds. The man you borrowed

1

from has sold the debt to the Earl of Nottingham, and the Earl would like to see you hang. You have a week to pay.'

Nottingham! Of course.

Defoe heard the door open and his wife stepped outside.

'Daniel, is there a problem?'

'Madam,' the man said with a false smile. 'Forgive the intrusion.' He seemed about to speak more – but before he could continue Defoe interrupted.

'Dearest heart, I beg you to go back inside. I shall be with you shortly.'

Sarah wavered. Their middle son came to the door, then their youngest daughter looked out too. Sarah looked back and caught sight of their anxious faces – then stepped back into the house, closing the door behind her.

'You have a week,' the man repeated.

'A week! Impossible.'

The man put his hand on his sword.

'I have no sword, but if you give me a minute to fetch one I shall fight you or any man.'

The man let go of the sword. 'I don't mean to fight you now. But we have found you, and we shall come armed next week to remove you. You shall hang. Your wife must find work in service. Your son must go to sea. And your daughter . . .' He paused. 'Well, we can help you to find work for her.'

'You threaten me, sir?'

'The Earl wants his money. And he shall have it.'

'I have powerful friends.'

The man sneered. 'But for how long can Oxford continue to help you? His power is draining away. He may lose the white staff tomorrow.'

This hit a nerve. Defoe exploded. 'Are you no Christian? What kind of man are you, to do this? To threaten a man, his wife and his children. Have you no feelings? No sense of what is right? The Lord looks down in judgement on us all . . .'

'They told me you have a way with words, sir. My work is valuable to the man who pays me. Look to yourself, sir. You have overspent, sir. You don't know how to live your life within your means. The work you do is worthless. Nobody wants what you have to sell, sir. I tell you once more: find the money in a week, or you shall hear from me again.'

*

Hours later, the devil pushed the man's words round and round Defoe's head while Sarah slept soundly beside him. Was it true? Defoe had once felt certain that people valued him, and his work. More recently, he felt less confident. How could he possibly raise the necessary money in a week?

It simply would not have occurred to him, then, that he could share his difficulty with his wife. So he kept it to himself. And he wondered at times if he might turn lunatic, fit only for Bedlam.

Carefully, he slid his legs out of bed on to the bare wooden floorboards and spread his fingers out before him, so that he would not bump into anything. He stood up straight. He knew the rooms well enough, after two months in this new home, and had taken care the night before not to leave anything on the floor.

He moved towards the wall, and, using his hands, felt ahead for the cupboard in which he had piled his clothes neatly so he could find them in the darkness.

A floorboard creaked beneath his foot and he stopped moving

3

for a moment, to be sure his wife had not woken. She didn't stir. So he opened the cupboard door and counted the items in the heap of clothes to be sure he left nothing. Then he felt underneath the cupboard for his buckled shoes and, clutching the lot to his chest, he slid along the wall to the door.

He knew the latch would make a noise, but there was nothing he could do – on retiring to bed Sarah insisted on closing it, to reduce any chance of their talking disturbing the children next door.

He put the clothes on the floor with the shoes on top, and carefully felt for the latch. It made a loud scraping sound, so he stood still again and listened for his wife, then when he was confident she still slept he picked up his pile of clothes and walked on to the landing.

But here he kicked by chance against some object – a child's shoe? – which clattered noisily across the wooden floor. He cursed, then asked God's forgiveness, felt renewed contempt for himself, and started moving carefully – his feet sweeping the floor gently for any other surprises – towards the stairs.

At the bottom, his feet felt the cold of the stone floor. He placed his bundle on the stairs and started to dress. But still he moved silently because sometimes his sister, if she couldn't fall asleep with the youngest children upstairs, retired to the rocking chair in the kitchen. Despite the full moon, Defoe could see nothing because he'd taken the precaution of closing the shutters against intruders.

Having dressed, he picked up his shoes – which would make too much noise if he wore them – and tiptoed to the window by the door. He placed them out of the way, and then turned behind him to feel for the kitchen table.

Usually there was a candle to be found there somewhere, but he couldn't feel anything, so he crept around the table, feeling his way from one chair back to the next, going the long way around to avoid the rocking chair, just in case, and finally reached the shelf where the candles and candlesticks were kept. He took out his tinder box and struck for light.

At that moment a sound of movement told him that someone was in the room with him. He abandoned the idea of lighting a candle, for now, but took one with him towards the front door, and having opened it, he stepped outside.

Here, the full moon blazed over his garden – there was enough light to read by, if he'd needed to. He lit the candle and went back inside. It flickered – cheap candles! What would his father have said! – but gave enough light to show him his sister. Poor thing, he thought. She can't stay here much longer. She too must be turned out to find work. At her age! There was always someone who needed a governess, or a lady's maid. But let's not think about that. The problem could still be avoided.

He walked past her more swiftly this time, towards a high shelf where he had hidden a key. He put the key in his pocket, and went towards the pantry, where three chests stood by the door. For safe-keeping, he kept his papers in the bottom one, so had first to remove the ones above in which his wife had used to store, among other things, scraps of cloth she'd managed to save, and hoped one day to stitch into a bedcover as a wedding gift for their oldest girl. It would not be long now.

In the bottom chest, he found a great heap of printed papers. They were bound together with ribbon and fixed with a wax seal, so he snapped it open to check that these were the papers he needed.

As he started to open the paper – a broadsheet – he thought he heard a creaking floorboard upstairs. He stood motionless again, watching his sister sleeping with her mouth slightly open, and waited to hear more. But again everything seemed to be still. Perhaps someone had woken, and risen to use their pot, then got back in bed.

He opened up the broadsheet. In large letters, its title read, 'What if the Queen Should Die?' He cast his eye over the smaller text below.

The Queen raises no money without Act of Parliament, keeps up no standing army in time of peace, disseizes no man of his property or estate: but every man sits in safety under his own vine and his fig-tree; and we shall do for as long as Her Majesty lives. BUT what if the Queen should die? The safety and the lasting happiness of the nation is so far secured, BUT what if the Queen should die? The Queen is mortal, tho' crowned with all that flattering courtiers can bring together, to make her appear Great, Glorious, Famous or what you please; yes, the Queen, yea, the Queen herself, is mortal and MUST die. None of us know how near the fatal blow may befall us: today it may come, while the cavilling reader is objecting against our putting this question and calling it needless and unreasonable; while the word is in thy very mouth mayest thou hear the fatal and melancholy news, the Queen is dead. Now that must at one time or other be heard. How can anyone say then that it is improper to ask what shall be our case? What shall we do, or what shall be done with us, if the Queen should DIE? The people of Britain want only to be shewed what imminent danger they are in — how much their safety and felicity depends upon the life of Her Majesty and what a state of confusion, distress and all sorts of dreaded calamities they will fall into at Her Majesty's death, if something be not done to settle them before her death.

It was urgent when he wrote it, and it was even more urgent today. Who could say if she would live another week?

He felt tears in his eyes. Ridiculous! But the loss of a monarch is no ordinary upheaval, for the relationship of the queen to her subjects is like that of a mother to her children. Without her, life could never be the same. And for Defoe, as for many others, everything depended on what happened next.

And on who should be king. Some three inches from the top was an engraving, showing a young man in fine clothes with a long face and full lips. 'A true likeness of the Pretender', it said beneath. He had stared at this picture so often, and for so long, in order to imprint it on his memory, that it had started to invade his dreams.

He folded the paper and put it back into the bundle, which he squeezed into his saddlebag by the door. He went to fetch his goose-feather quill – very short now – and wrapped that carefully, along with a jar of ink. Then he closed the chest, replaced the other chests on top, and went to fetch his weapons.

Chapter 2

The Cause of the Righteous

In the garden, Defoe walked to the old plum tree. Among its branches he found the spade he had hidden there on Sunday. He walked towards the wall farthest from the house and found a prickly gooseberry bush.

He had planted the bush himself, soon after they moved here, working at night as he did now. Any bush would do, but the prickles provided a useful means to keep people away from what was buried beneath it.

He had bare hands, and felt the sharp pain of the prickles against his skin as he used the spade to lift the bush. He put it carefully to one side and started to dig.

Even at the old house, with all the space inside, he had kept this particular chest buried in the garden. It was easier that way to hide it from the servants. Now there were no servants – they'd all been dismissed when the money ran out – but there was nowhere to hide a big chest from his family either.

It didn't take long to reach the top of the chest, but digging around it, carefully, was a slow process. He knew he could not keep this same chest underground much longer, it was already rotting, but he felt attached to it. He'd been given it by a pirate who needed help writing a letter. 'This chest has been around the world,' the pirate had said. 'Use it well, and it will bring you luck.'

After fifteen minutes, he was able to pull the chest out of the ground. He felt in his pocket for the key, and unlocked it. The lock had rusted, so it would not open. He poked at the rust with the key, and banged on the side of the chest, conscious that the noise might wake someone but having little alternative, and hoping that the plum tree might muffle the sound.

At last, the chest opened. Inside it was a pistol, and a bag containing powder and balls. He took them out and wondered where to put them. He should have brought out his greatcoat, with pockets so big they could hide anything – but he had not. So he tied the bag to the keychain at his waist and shoved the pistol into the top of his breeches, pirate fashion. Reaching down into the chest again, he pulled out a box containing a small jar of arsenic. He checked the jar for any sign it might be broken, and put it in his pocket. Then he pulled out a roll of cloth, which he carefully unrolled to reveal, inside, a handsome sword in a simple scabbard.

He put this on the floor beside him and found a belt inside the chest. And that was all he needed. He locked the chest again, lowered it back into the ground and filled the hole with the undamaged gooseberry bush.

Each of these weapons had been given him by somebody he had come to respect – somebody who had later been killed as a result of their attachment to the cause of the righteous. They were no longer alive to carry out that work, but he could do it for them.

The pistol was something he had been given in Somerset, on his way home from the disastrous Monmouth Rebellion. A rebel by the name of Leonard Digges had found it in the hands of a dead trooper in the King's army, and had then taken to hiding in long grass while great fires burned all around.

'Stop, friend!' he said when Defoe ran past. 'Here's a pistol. They're hanging any rebels they find.'

'Thank you, friend.' Defoe stopped running and hid in the grass beside the man. He had not recognised him yet.

'You're Daniel Defoe. We spoke before the battle. I'm Leonard Digges.'

'Do not use my real name,' Defoe replied. 'Call me Moreton. And here – take one of these bags. I found them. They're full of hosiery. I'm selling them from house to house. Let me do the talk-ing.' And that's when Digges had given him the pistol.

The sword was a gift from a Scotsman, grateful for his work preparing the Scots for the Act of Union – a friend who would later be torn to pieces by the savage mob in Edinburgh.

But this sword had not been sharpened for years, if ever. Sharp-ening it now was, obviously, out of the question – far too loud – but perhaps he might find a stone and sharpen it on his journey.

He took the sword from its sheath and waved it in the air before him, as if fighting an imaginary enemy. Then he swung it at the gooseberry bush, which bent and snapped beneath the blow. He cringed at the noise, as he wondered exactly how sharp the sword really was.

Hoping to find out, he wandered round the garden under the full moon, looking for a better target. And his eye fell on the cab-bages.

He stood before them and thought of beheading them. He remembered riding with Digges through the towns in Somerset, watching scenes of unimaginable cruelty. 'See how this Catholic king loves his subjects,' Digges said. Defoe remembered one particular trooper, who seemed to take great pleasure in torturing rebel farmers and their young sons before hanging them, slicing off their ears, and noses, and cutting out their guts while they still lived. Defoe would happily have killed the man to put an end to it.

The cabbages were too low to swing at. So he got down on his knees, then took in a deep breath and — swoosh — he cut the head off the nearest one. The sword cut through cleanly. He lifted the cabbage with one hand and held it up as if he were inspecting the severed head of that black-hearted trooper.

And then his wife's voice from just behind him said, 'Daniel, what are you doing to those cabbages?'

He dropped the sword and the cabbage and leapt to his feet. He turned to see Sarah's silhouette — the moon was behind her. He could not imagine what to say.

'And where did you get that sword?'

*

Defoe's friends told him he should have known better than to marry a girl with a dowry. A man like him should have married an honest woman who knew poverty first-hand, because otherwise he would always be indebted to her, as indeed he was.

Even leaving aside the dowry he had wasted, he knew himself lucky to have married such a woman — a shining light in the paths of righteousness. The pretty young thing he'd wed decades before had proved a loving mother to their handsome and obedient children, two of them now parents themselves; and with him too Sarah was patient and encouraging; perhaps more so. She always supported his projects, no matter how outlandish, and forgave the consequences, all too often catastrophic. As a girl she had grown up in comfort – more comfortable, at any rate, than she'd been since she married him, even when he had been at the height of his commercial success – but she never complained. This patient, cheerful endurance was harder on him than a less forgiving woman's reproaches might have been. It required him likewise to put on a brave face, when what he really wanted to say was: 'What about me? Don't you think my failures have hurt me too?' Instead, every morning on waking, after thanking his Creator, he would kiss Sarah's forehead and tell her that today he would make up to her, and to the children, everything he'd put them through. He would buy back what they had lost, build a new home, clothe them all properly and – most importantly – give Sarah the rest and tranquillity she deserved. But he had to act at once, before it was too late. In another ten years even the youngest of the children would have left home and Sarah would be an old woman. She'd grown thin, already her hair was grey and the ankle she had broken many years ago, carrying one of the children downstairs, troubled her more than ever.

To see the woman you love in difficulty, to be unable to relieve her, and to know that you have brought her to this situation, is a horror that nobody can imagine till they feel it themselves. Defoe put on at all times an air of cheerful resolution, but it was hard, sometimes, to fend off the sensation, suffocating already and getting stronger by the day, that the best of his life was already behind him.

Lately, he saw in her parents and even sometimes in the unguarded expressions of his children, particularly his oldest boy, hints of disappointment and even resentment that were more pain-ful than outright reproach.

He had tried many trades. Most recently, with help from his father-in-law, he'd been a merchant in tobacco, beer, wine, silks, muslins, cochineal, wax, dates, tea and ostrich feathers. He bought from Portugal and America and resold across Britain. But gradually he'd accumulated vast debts, and borrowed from others in order to repay them. He pledged and pawned, sold his goods at a loss, all the while hoping for one spectacular trade to liberate him – to pay off everybody at once. Earlier this year, he sustained the heaviest blow: a consignment of Maryland tobacco was captured by French pirates. The ship's master had declined to pay protec- tion money to his naval escort, which responded by pressing into service a good portion of the crew, and the remainder was unable to protect the cargo when pirates appeared. Suddenly unable to repay his creditors, Defoe was bankrupted and imprisoned, for the vast sum of £17,000. The business was taken from him, the servants dismissed and the family ejected from their house. He himself was thrown into debtor's prison, not once but three times, by creditors who refused to agree on how best to deal with him.

Despite being a proud man, he'd been obliged to get out, even- tually, by sending his eldest son to plead for money from the Lord Treasurer, the Earl of Oxford, who had once been kind enough to notice something Defoe wrote. It was a desperate measure, unlikely to produce results. But Oxford showed greater kindness than Defoe had dared to hope for, and by handing over the necessary sum, the Lord Treasurer earned his everlasting loyalty. 'My lord,' Defoe promised Oxford at the time. 'I shall always be your most devoted supporter, pleased to serve you in any way I can.'

With that promise in mind, he'd written to Oxford with a specific proposal, but had heard nothing for weeks. It was said, though nobody could remember who proposed it first, that the law of inertia was the law of nature that had the most devastating effect on the Lord Treasurer, but Defoe could wait no more. He was desperate. He had to do something.

*

'I got it from a friend.'

'What friend?'

'How long have you been watching?'

He walked around her so that she turned her head and he could see her expression in the moonlight.

'Daniel, what are you doing?'

He couldn't possibly tell her the truth. Not after all these years, no matter how much he wished he could. It would be too great a shock. She would never again believe anything he told her.

'I have to go on a journey. I am taking a sword because I shall be mixing with people who have pretensions of quality.'

'Who gave it to you? What friend?'

'A man named Murray. He was a friend to me when I was working in Scotland.'

'Is that a pistol in your belt? Gentlemen don't carry pistols like that. Only highwaymen, and privateers, and boys at their games. What kind of people are going on this journey? Tell me, Daniel. Please. Tell me the truth.'

She had never spoken to him like that – not once in all these years had she given any hint of suspicion or distrust. What could he say?

'We live in dangerous times, my sweet.'

'Tell me, Daniel. Tell me about the pistol.'

'I have never used it.'

'Where did you get it?'

'In the West Country.'

There was a very long silence. Defoe could hold a silence as well as any horse trader, but this was agony.

'Daniel, I have never asked you before, but tell me truthfully, did you fight for the Duke of Monmouth?'

He was astonished. In all their marriage she had said nothing.

'If I said yes, that would be to admit treason.'

'I knew it. How could you be so foolish?'

'Our cause was just. We were fighting to rid the country of a Catholic tyrant.'

'It didn't work. If you had fallen into the hands of the King's troops your children would have lost their father.'

She had little idea of how nearly that had happened. Defoe refused to admit anything directly. But he felt an overwhelming sadness.

'They might have been better off,' he said.

'Oh, Daniel.' She moved towards him and took his hand.

'Why did you wake?'

'Why are you stealing about in the early hours like this? What have I done that you should keep it secret? For a fortnight you have been distracted. You pay no attention when the children speak to you. If I disturb you, you wave me away. You hardly eat, and last night you muttered in your sleep. You talked about courage, and fighting, and groaned about the Lord's people stretched out hang-ing by the roadsides. I wiped the sweat from your face and shook you but you only shouted curses at the King. I stopped shaking you for fear you'd wake the little ones . . . there is something awful on your mind. You must tell me what it is.'

She got down on her knees, still clutching his hand. 'Please, tell me.'

'My sweet, please don't kneel.' He helped her up. 'Don't ask where I'm going, or what I'm doing. I can't tell you, but I beg you to trust me. I have work to do for the Earl of Oxford – a great man, and upright. I have never had any work that was more important.'

Throughout his career, alongside the more conventional forays into commerce, spycraft and writing were the two things that brought him the most satisfaction. Before the union with Scotland, he had travelled extensively north of the border, investigating the views of the natives. That work, which Oxford told him had resulted in the deaths of other agents before him, greatly facilitated the Act of Union – to Scotland's disadvantage, as many there now realised. But he'd told Sarah he went to Scotland for trade, and had merely used the opportunity to write a little while he was there. For several years he had written and published his own newspaper, the *Review*, which provided a forum for his opinions and also sold well. Indeed, his greatest financial success to date was the poem he wrote in celebration of the mongrel origins of the English, written in defence of the Queen's immediate predecessor, her Dutch-born brother-in-law William of Orange. 'The True-Born Englishman' was extensively reprinted, and Defoe had had the pleasure of hearing people repeat it in his presence.

'I saw a heap of papers in your saddle bags,' Sarah said. 'Are you planning to publish another dangerous pamphlet?'

He had published many pamphlets, but he knew what she was referring to.

'I have learned my lesson.'

'I wish I could be sure.'

16

In his most popular satire, 'The Shortest Way with Dissenters', Defoe had written under an assumed name that the solution to the problem of the Nonconformists was to put them to death. But this had failed to register as satirical — most readers assumed that it was a serious suggestion, only marginally beyond the bounds of what was acceptable. Despite being Nonconformist himself, Defoe was prosecuted by the cruel Earl of Nottingham, and on conviction he was put in the stocks, on market day, to have missiles and abuse hurled at him. Then he was fined and imprisoned.

'My love, you must trust me.'

'Promise me you will not hurt anybody. Your soul is in the balance, Daniel.'

'Let's go inside,' he said, ignoring her request. 'You can help me to pack and leave before the others wake up.'

*

He started his journey to Windsor before sunrise. His Elizabethan costume finally folded neatly away in his saddlebags, he pulled a hat low over his face and tucked a pair of pistols inside his horse-man's coat, 'borrowed' long ago from a corporal in Marlborough's army.

He slipped a light scarf around his neck and hid inside his shirt the bottle filled with arsenic, with which he might either poison a man's food or impregnate his clothes. Then he mounted his horse, a chestnut mare he shared with a fellow who worshipped at his temple. Sarah took his hand. 'I really don't know what I would do if something awful happened to you.'

He crossed the fields dividing Islington from London while they were still covered in darkness. In the city, he'd found little sign of life: windows stood open against the hot summer nights, but from only a few did faint candlelight flicker, where families watched over the sick or dying. Otherwise, all was still.

At five o'clock he rode close by a nightwatchman as he yelled the time on a street corner; and shortly after glimpsed what appeared in the half-light to be a duel – the sound of gunfire and the sudden collapse of one silhouetted figure. He kept moving, as if he'd seen nothing. Gradually the streets began to fill with market carts and shutters came up on the public houses. Defoe kept riding, hoping to remain unnoticed.

The memory of old king James made Defoe cry out in his sleep

Chapter 3

Everybody is Waiting For Me to Die

Queen Anne was looking forward to this evening's ball, the first such event to spur her excitement in years. After all, its historical theme – England's glorious Elizabethan past – was her own idea.

The Queen rose no later than usual, at 10 a.m., prayed, then took breakfast in her chamber: a dozen wheat cakes, two hard-boiled goose eggs, several slices of tongue, pigeon pie, good salted herring, fried kidneys, and a dish of pease pottage – all rinsed through with the best Trumpington ale. After that, she smoked a pipe, which induced a lengthy fit of coughing. The Queen was in her fifties, vastly overweight, and unwell. Her bedchamber woman Abigail, Lady Masham, waited nervously for the fit to pass.

Another lady-in-waiting, Mary Arden, took the Queen's hand.

'Mary, why can't you do something useful?' said Lady Masham. 'Go and fetch Dr Arbuthnot.'

The doctor adjusted his wig as he entered, muttering apologies for his slowness. By that time, the coughing had ceased. He examined her briefly.

'Everybody is waiting for me to die,' the Queen told him. 'They want me to do something decisive.'

He couldn't think of a good way to tell her that she was not going to live much longer. So he pretended not to have heard her, peered at her tongue, asked if she felt at all light/headed, then pronounced her well. Well enough, at any rate, to attend the ball. 'And if I may say so, the whole court looks forward to your imper/ sonation of Queen Elizabeth.'

The Queen had been in Windsor for some weeks. Twelve years had passed since the start of her glorious reign. Sunshine gently warmed the park, the forest and the castle. Lately, as if she could do nothing else, the Queen contemplated death, and weighed the merits of making some bold gesture with regard to the succession, and considered which of the two leading candidates should bene/ fit from such a gesture – and finally she wondered whether it was not really all too much trouble after all, best left for others to deter/ mine after she had gone.

Meanwhile her subjects got on with the ordinary business of life. In the country, they sat under large oaks and elms, gorging themselves on summer fruits, playing the Jew's harp and singing smutty ballads. In spa towns such as Bath and Buxton, they virtuously sipped whole pints of the sulphurous waters in which, not long before, they had bathed their scrofulous skins; at Scar/ borough and Brighthelmstone they did much the same with seawater. In London, a day's ride from Windsor, those who were not unfortunately manacled inside one of the capital's many prisons and mad houses diverted themselves with cockfighting; drinking gin until the limbs and eyeballs lost their function; travelling to and from assignations in closed sedan chairs; striking bargains with tradesmen; talking politics in coffee houses, or else trading jests from the latest plays, and spoiling them with too much repeating; begging on street corners; stealing purses; singing psalms; smoking pipes and dreaming of a better life in the East Indies or the American colonies; calling on neighbours at home and taking tea with them for hours on end; riding in Hyde Park; playing the lottery, or the viola; and giving birth with no more anaesthetic than a bottle of brandy.

But for many of the most important people, and those who depended on them – particularly those who had travelled with the court to Windsor – it was difficult to concentrate on the ordinary business of life because so much depended on the future of the crown. The Queen had no living offspring and the men most likely to inherit – both based overseas – were preparing either to accept the crown graciously or to fight for it if necessary. Officially, it seemed clear who would get it – the Act of Settlement ensured that no Catholic could inherit – but shocking things had occurred before now. Few people at court knew which prince to support, publicly, at any rate, though naturally both would be offered support in private. The only certainty was that in a few months – perhaps just weeks, or days – the Queen would no longer be alive to promote her favourites or keep down those they opposed. Tory ministers asserted that the Queen was, in fact, in good health, while papers favourable to the opposition went as far as to announce that she was dead already. Against this uncertainty, bank stock had fallen four per cent.

Suddenly it seemed important again to be seen at court, and to cultivate useful alliances. Years had passed since so many last attended. Parliament was reluctant to give the invalid Queen an allowance for entertainment and, even if she had been able to walk across the room unaided, her court would have been duller than many could have wished; Anne's outlook was far removed from the gaudy excesses of the past, when King Charles's cavaliers drunkenly fucked in corridors and unburdened their bowels wherever they could find a corner not already used for that purpose. Few houses in England, belonging to persons of quality, were kept more privately than Anne's court. Wits liked to say that it served 'just about satisfactorily' as a coffee house, and coffee houses served much better as a court. They took more pleasure from political clubs – such as the Cocoa Tree (for the Tories) and the Kit Kat (for the Whigs) – or from the great country houses. After all, aside from the supposedly edifying sight of Her Majesty herself – when that, increasingly rarely, was available – the court had little to recommend it. 'Nothing but ceremony,' people said. 'No conversation. You play cards after dinner, drink tea, bow extremely and return home.'

Now, even those mild activities had come to seem slightly dangerous for the invalid queen. For much of the afternoon she, Lady Masham and Lady Mary had played cards; a few hands of quadrille, then cribbage, basset and finally piquet when the other games bored them. They stopped every so often for a plate of jellies or a dish of green tea – and each time the Queen seemed to swallow something the wrong way, and splutter painfully, so that everybody's heart stopped until she breathed easily again.

They played for small stakes, but by four o'clock Lady Masham was down several shillings, and Mary, preoccupied by the imminent arrival at court of her sweetheart, had done substantially worse; neither woman was unhappy to start what promised to be a lengthy toilet.

They began by helping the Queen towards her lacquered dressing table. She moved heavily, one arm over each woman's shoulders. Here, they spent several moments admiring the bright red wig, resting on a tall stand, which had been specially prepared for her to hint at the gingerish majesty of her predecessor. 'It's frightful!' said Lady Masham cheerfully.

With some assistance from the distracted Mary – and with Her Majesty's permission – Lady Masham started to undress the Queen. First she removed the nightgown, then the undergarments and with great difficulty addressed the cap tied beneath her chin. The knot was lost between the rolls of fat on her neck, so Lady Masham pulled firmly on the ends, but this only seemed to tighten it. Once again seeking permission, she took a couteau from the table and cut the cords altogether. Finally, Lady Masham unsaddled the Queen's spectacles and Her Majesty blinked blindly at nothing. Lady Masham stood back momentarily to take in fully the great mass of pale fat, topped by a head that shone with perspiration through her thin hair. Not quite inaudibly, Lady Masham sighed.

Sometimes Mary used to wonder if Lady Masham was being deliberately unkind towards the Queen. But she said nothing. As time passed she became increasingly convinced of Lady Masham's – there was no other word – cruelty. But what could she do about it?

At that moment, while the Queen was still sitting entirely naked, the First Lady of the Bedchamber, the Duchess of Somerset, scratched at the door then stepped inside without waiting for a reply. 'Your Majesty,' she began, not bothering to curtsey to the unseeing monarch. 'I came to ask if I might help with your preparations – but I see you are well looked after.' Strictly speaking, the Duchess should have supervised the Queen's toilet, but she graciously delegated this honour to Lady Masham. Consequently, the Duchess had no idea of the fits, the cramps, the uncontrolled flatulence, the cracked lips, the eyes that gummed together while the Queen slept, the copious dandruff, the stench of her false teeth, the suppurating sores on her legs, and back, and her private parts.

'Yes, Abigail is very good to me,' the Queen replied. 'But, oh, I hate to sit in front of the mirror. I was never a beauty, but it pains me beyond measure to see the ruin I have become.'

Nobody spoke, until the Queen added: 'Have you any news about the ball?'

*

The regulars at court noted a distinct feeling of nervous excitement this evening. Carriages blocked the streets of Windsor, all along Church Street and Thames Street, for nearly a mile from the castle. Sedan chairs, drenched inside and out after the heavy rainfall, weaved their solitary passengers between chaises and chariots. Horses whinnied unhappily. Drivers obscenely yodelled. Meanwhile, the occupants of the gaudily painted coaches – with six matching horses, footmen on the back and postboys riding with the first pair, all decked out in matching uniforms – pretended not to have any part of it. 'Don't look out of the window, Henrietta,' a mother might have said. 'You only encourage them to look back.'

Rather than wait for the traffic to clear, some of the men and women inside those gridlocked carriages stepped down to walk. At Wren's new town hall a few of them pointed out the statue of Anne on the north façade. Small boys from Windsor chewing tobacco, earned pennies by offering to carry the ladies' heavy skirts over the wet streets, filthy with sodden manure. Those who had just arrived, upon running into old friends, compared the houses they had taken, the superiority of the drawing rooms, the style of the fittings and the furniture; and who had come to visit them, each boasting of the great number of visitors' cards left at their doors by people of whom they knew nothing. At the gates, they pressed through a scrum of bold beggars; girls with babes on each breast, wooden-legged sailors and blind boys in rags who cursed like infantrymen.

Back in the Queen's chambers, the Duchess intended to find out at once, she said, whether any unexpected arrivals – or unexpected absences – had been reported. She would report back as soon as she knew more. Taking a good look at Mary, she pronounced that she became prettier by the day, and who knows, she might one day soon be the prettiest girl in England – a comment that Lady Masham affected not to hear. Then the Duchess quit the room, with no more formality than she arrived.

Lady Masham slipped an under-bodice over the Queen's head. Next she strapped on the whalebone corset, pulling violently again and again as she tightened it, while Mary held the Queen's hands to stop her being tugged off the stool. Then Lady Masham took a petticoat and knelt on the wooden floor before the Queen to slip it over her feet, one at a time, then hoist it on to her thighs. With much effort, the Queen rose from her stool so that Lady Masham could hitch the petticoat into position on the royal waist. This process was repeated for each additional petticoat – there were eight altogether – and again for the farthingale that went over them.

'I'm sorry,' said the Queen. 'It's all going to have to come off again. I need my pot.'

Lady Masham found the porcelain pot, and with Mary beside her she slipped outside the room. She dismissed the footmen with a nod and pressed her ear to the door, only too conscious that the

Queen's uncle, King Charles, had suffered a catastrophic stroke while carrying out his private business.

'I have finished!' the Queen called eventually, and her women stepped back inside. Lady Masham placed a cloth over the copious, sweet-smelling burden of the chamberpot and passed it to a footman to carry away for inspection by Doctor Arbuthnot.

An hour or so later, Lady Masham had managed to dress the Queen entirely, and to make substantial progress on her face: painting it all over with white lead, applying crimson in large, precise circles on the cheeks, then gumming into place, high on the forehead, the first of two eyebrows made of mouse fur.

Meanwhile, Lady Mary looked at a letter she kept folded in her pocket. She opened the letter carefully. Like the others that had come before, it was signed 'Your dear friend Hannah Holland', the same name inscribed on the envelope beneath the seal. It began with three paragraphs of chat about idle subjects, more or less identical to the opening of previous letters. When Mary was younger she'd been close friends with Hannah, and for years they'd sustained a daily correspondence full of brilliant ideas. Then Hannah died — of smallpox — but the letters kept coming. The writer revealed that he had, in fact, been drafting Hannah's letters for several months before she died, for her to copy out before sending. He also revealed his identity: it was Hannah's older brother, Samuel. And he declared himself a passionate admirer. His letters enchanted her: she simply couldn't help falling in love with the man who wrote them. She had few opportunities to meet him in person, but when they did meet she was more than satisfied. As she wrote in her journal, Samuel was tall and had a pleasing countenance, intelligent eyes, and lively conversation. If he was not absolutely the most handsome man in England, he was very near it. But Mary had no mother to guide her and knew her father would be devastated if he found out she loved a man from such a family as Samuel's, one that had dipped its hands in royal blood.

By longstanding arrangement, the letter's most interesting passages started from the fourth paragraph onwards. On the third page, there was a poem. She read it fast, then again more slowly, and then a third time.

If I could stop the Clocks, I'd stop them here,
The Finny Tribe would no more swim, than if
The Ocean froze; and supple Beasts go stiff
As if their Bones and Tendons turned to Stone.
Halt now the Transit of the Sun and Spheres.
No Candles burn away, nor Fashions change.
Be Nothing new, and Nothing therefore strange.
Postpone, for good, Contention o'er the Throne,
The Queen shall never die, and Time shall smile
On her, bow low like Frenchmen at Versailles.
Just one thing change: your Father think me his,
No less contented by you than he is.
Stop turning, World! Let Queen and Father bless,
For Mary, when I begged her hand, said Yes.

It may not have been the best poem she had ever read, but it was the first poem that was written for her. She folded it up, kissed both sides, and placed it in a pocket.

It was true! She had agreed to marry Samuel. Writing to accept his proposal had been the most difficult thing she'd ever done. She was thrilled that he loved her enough to ask – his family was unlikely to approve – and she loved him without reservation. But the engagement would destroy her father. Several times she had broken off writing to shed tears over the page, and had to start over again.

The Duchess reappeared. 'Your Majesty,' she began. 'This promises to be the most successful ball you have ever had the wisdom to devise. The entire town is full, so full that I would not previously have believed it possible. Even the best families, if they arrived late, have been unable to secure lodgings. Some have taken rooms as far away as Slough. It seems we shall see people tonight we have not so much as glimpsed for years.'

After a pause, she added, 'Some of them, I daresay, would hardly be given admittance if the footmen at the door could only tell who they were. Who knows what strangers might appear.'

She was thinking of somebody she'd met a few months previously, a funny little woman who had dedicated to Queen Anne her book about Britain's Saxon past. The Duchess hardly knew what to say, particularly when she learned that this scarecrow intended to present herself at the ball – and, what was worse, threatened to dance for the court in the Saxon fashion.

But the Duchess didn't actually spell out that this was the sort of stranger she had in mind. Consequently, her offhand remark allowed for a more sinister interpretation that would have astonished her.

'And it seems that Oxford and Bolingbroke intend to appear together, to end Walpole's talk of their having fallen out.'

The Queen smiled, but she was hardly listening. It had not previously occurred to her that unexpected visitors might appear. Now she could hardly think of anything else. Her heart began to throb. She broke into a sweat. She worried that one particular stranger – not seen by her since he was a baby – might be brought near, perhaps disguised as somebody else, then suddenly spring himself upon her.

She became oblivious of the women around her, and started talking to her son, William, who was sitting quietly on the windowseat nearby. He was a handsome young man, very like his father to look at.

'I know that everybody expects me to die soon,' the Queen told him, 'and that nobody will miss me much. All they want is for me to make some decisive statement, before it's too late, about the succession.'

She fell silent.

'But if they tried that tonight — at my first public appearance for weeks — I don't think I could bear it.'

William said nothing. He would so much have liked to think of the right words to soothe his dear mother, but words failed him.

*

And so it was that, less than fifteen minutes after the Duchess's second appearance, the Queen found she was feeling unwell. She shivered. She became conscious of indigestion flaming high up in her chest. St Anthony's Fire streaked across her arms. The sweat on her forehead grew from tiny beads to large drops and finally heavy streams — which washed the mingled white and red powders off her face and on to her neck.

She asked to be undressed again, apologising to Lady Masham for putting her to so much trouble. She sent Mary to fetch some brandy, which Mary spilled over her ('Oh, Mary!'), and then to extinguish the candles. Finally, dressed in her nightclothes once more, she took up her position by the window, surrounded by all her handsome sons and beautiful daughters, and watched closely for the certain person she feared.

Queen Anne hated to sit in front of a mirror

Chapter 4

The Greatest Master of Intelligence

When he was sure the Treasurer was home, Defoe knocked on the door and asked the servant for a meeting with his master.

'His Lordship is not home.'

'I know he is. I saw him coming and going this morning.'

'He can't be disturbed.'

'My business is urgent. He will thank you for letting me in.'

'Tell me what your business is, and I shall give him a message when he is free. Come back tomorrow.'

'I can tell this business to nobody except him.'

'He is dining.'

'With his family. Nobody else. I have been watching for some time. I don't wish to be insolent, or to presume, but this is a state matter of the greatest importance. I can wait until he has eaten. But please let me in.'

The man refused, but Defoe refused to be budged. This could be his only chance. Eventually Oxford came to see who it was that required such urgent attention. He carried a young child with him, a granddaughter perhaps, and seemed at first greatly put out. But his frown softened when he recognised Defoe, whom he greeted as a loyal servant of the ministry and a friend of the righteous. Defoe capitalised on this promising development by pulling a face to make the little girl laugh – ears out, eyes crossed – a face that had never failed to amuse his own children at that age. Once again, it produced the desired effect.

'What mission brings you here so urgently?' Oxford asked, ushering Defoe into a private room with papers piled high on every available surface. The little girl had reverted to frowning at the uninvited guest.

'My lord, as I love you, I hope you will forgive the intrusion. I have written to you several times but know well that you are burdened with too many correspondents. I have come to explain a project that would serve you well, particularly at a time as uncertain as this.'

Oxford set down the grim child and sent her to rejoin her father at dinner.

Defoe saw the Lord Treasurer, as he'd told him before, as a man with the potential to eclipse Cardinal Richelieu and King Gustavus Adolphus as the greatest master of intelligence of the age. 'My Lord, you are greater even than Elizabeth's spymaster, Sir Francis Walsingham, whose network of informers detected the treason of Mary, Queen of Scots, and uncovered Spanish plans for the Armada.'

Defoe knew how to flatter, but in this he was sincere. According to his calculations, which he had taken care to write out in a fair script, a hundred thousand pounds per annum spent now for three years would be the best money the nation ever laid out, with merchants appointed as spies in Scotland and France, particularly around the enemy's principal naval bases. Defoe would not do all the work, but would himself put together a perfect list of all the gentry and family of rank in England, their residence, character and political faction; all the clergy, their character and morals; and the leading men in the cities and boroughs, their commercial interests and the parties they supported.

Defoe had made a study of the most persuasive words in English and made sure to include each one. He spoke of making discoveries, offered guarantees, said his results were proven, that they would save money and, finally, that they would secure safety for all Her Majesty's loyal subjects.

'In gathering information about the Pretender, I have already infiltrated fur-shops, booksellers and the bitterly rivalrous coffee shops of Covent Garden. I have posed as a French fencing master, a diamond-dealing Jew from Holland, and an importer of Spanish wines. As a result, I have found out a plot of the greatest threat to England since the Armada. The Queen's supposed half-brother, who claims the English throne as his own, intends to leave France and appear in person at the English court, known only to his most trusted supporters. There could hardly be a better opportunity for the Pretender than a costume ball such as tonight's, at which so many unfamiliar faces will also be present. But, my lord, I am ready. For weeks I have studied the Pretender's likeness, and I would recognise at once the long face, the bright eyes, the finger-thick lips.'

'This is impossible. The Pretender would not dare to come here. He would pay with his life if anybody recognised him.'

'I have the plot on good authority, my lord.'

'And what would you do if you saw him?'

'I have been among soldiers and mercenaries long enough, my lord, to learn a swift and tidy execution. As a Christian, I feel in my heart the truth of the Commandments, and value the lives of all God's children. But I would do what I have to do, as well as I know how, and then put it from my mind.'

'If it goes wrong?'

'Then my own life would be finished. I would never see my beloved wife and children again. But if I succeed, I will have achieved a greater thing than many of the greatest men in English history: to save the Queen's subjects from Catholic tyranny, perhaps for ever.'

Oxford said nothing, only once uncrossing his arms to remove the wig he'd put on to answer the door. His own hair, beneath it, was cropped short and dark grey, though Oxford – like Defoe a Nonconformist by background, and full of the leaven of true righteousness – had endured enough in the last few years to turn every hair white. He was still in mourning for his daughter.

Then he said: 'It may not be enough, Defoe, merely to gather information . . . It's an excellent idea. And there has never been a time that needed it more. It will cost money, a lot of money, and I can't be sure the Queen's treasury can afford that. You must allow me to think it over. In the meantime I must ask you to devote yourself to the task without those funds. You must improvise.'

Defoe was appalled, but years of habit had trained him to conceal his true feelings. He felt a physical pain in his stomach at the realisation he would likely earn nothing from Oxford. Another man might have pleaded, explained how desperate his situation had become, but Defoe was too firmly habituated to secrecy, and pride. Already, his mind was busy, planning something bold that might change Oxford's position. But what?

'We live in dangerous times,' Oxford continued. 'You mentioned the Armada. Well, in years to come I believe people will see that the threat to this country, and the people living here today, is no less grave than it was when the Spanish sent their ships against Queen Elizabeth.'

'Do you have information already, about the Pretender?'

Oxford rubbed his eye, breathed deeply and pinched the end of his nose. 'Your guess is as good as mine. Any Englishman who hopes to prevent the worst must take whatever steps are necessary – no matter what the cost to themselves. If you wish to attend the ball, I shall have you added to the guest list.'

A heaviness imposed itself on Defoe as he realised what Oxford required from him. The meeting had not gone as planned: there was to be no money, and his commission was more onerous than he had expected. He'd thought that bringing news of the Pretender would earn him a reward, and that other forces would be drafted in to take action against the imposter. Oxford offered Defoe nothing – unless he considered it a privilege for Defoe to despatch the Pretender himself.

'My lord, if I remove any threat from the Pretender, might I hope for some reward?'

'I can promise nothing.'

Defoe felt as if he had been punched in the stomach. He had confidence in his abilities, and by God's will he placed himself at the service of his patron, as a captain puts his sword into the hand of his sovereign, with which to lay waste his enemies. Their eyes locked in expressions of the utmost seriousness.

'I will do what I must, my lord.'

Oxford patted him on the shoulder. 'I know you will. I was reading something of yours yesterday.' From among the papers on his desk, Oxford picked up a copy of the *Review*. Defoe felt a surge of pride as Oxford read his words back to him.

'"Our men are the stoutest and best, because strip them naked from the waist upwards and give them no weapons at all but their hands and heels, and turn them into a room, or stage, and lock them in with the like number of other men of any nation, man for man, and they shall beat the best men you shall find in the world." These are fine words, Defoe, and true. I would not bet a farthing on the man locked in a room with you. But tell me, I have not seen the *Review* in a while. Are you still publishing?'

Defoe had put the paper out single-handed for nine years, but a year ago he had stopped. He didn't want to go into it, so he just shook his head, then asked: 'Might I impose just a little more, by requesting a drink. I have been travelling for many hours.'

Oxford went to the door and called for the maid. Waiting for her to bring some ale, he apologised for failing to offer something beforehand. 'I would ask you to dine with us, but . . .'

Defoe insisted that was unnecessary.

'You do look hungry. If you care to step downstairs among the servants I know they would feed you well . . .'

Defoe shook his head. 'Your Lordship has already been too kind.' The maid appeared with Defoe's drink, which he drank slowly at first and then, remembering that he was keeping Oxford away from his guests, with haste that caused it to spill down his front.

Oxford affected not to notice, and politely begged Defoe's forgiveness. 'But I really do need to rejoin my guests . . .'

Defoe bowed deeply, wiping foam from his upper lip, and thanked his patron once again. The maid showed him to the door.

Shortly afterwards, the same footman who had previously attempted to keep him out of the house came rushing after him. He carried a heavy parcel. 'Mr Defoe, sir!' the man called. 'I have a gift for you from the Lord Treasurer.'

It was a huge ham. The man delivered it without entirely elim-
inating from his manner the lofty, unhelpful tone he'd used earlier.
'His Lordship sends his compliments to Mrs Defoe and all the
little Defoes.'

Since the latest bankruptcy, the only meat he had tasted was
oxtails and sheep's trotters, and those only on special occasions.
More frequently the Defoe family sat down to a dinner of toasted
cheese. He shoved it into his saddlebag, and rode on.

*

By midday, he'd got as far as the village of Hammersmith. He
rested his horse, ate a bite or two of the ham, then hurried on – he
was terribly hungry, but could eat more later.

He was not sorry to leave London behind him, smelling fouler
than ever, what with two-day-old fish left over from market day
choking the gutters amid the usual mess of dead cats, mud, horse
dung, ashes, turnip tops, coal dust, and scraps of cloth stained
with excrement. He'd stopped early to take a few more bites of the
ham, and some ale, at Brentford before braving the dusty plains of
Hounslow Heath and the highwaymen who lurked there. He
murmured psalms under his breath as he crossed that dangerous
territory – sang praises lustily to the Lord – but encountered nothing more menacing than an Irish beggar, seemingly drunk. 'D'you
have any change, Sor?' the man slurred. Unwilling to take any
chances – he might have been using pretence – Defoe called the
beggar over and proffered a shilling. And as soon as he was close
enough he smashed the end of his pistol against the man's skull,
then rode off at speed in case he had an accomplice, begging forgiveness from God if the man had not deserved that blow.

After a quarter of a mile, Defoe looked behind him and saw the man lying on the ground. There was nobody else nearby. Slowly, carefully, he rode over to the man to find him on his back, bleeding from his ear, with vomit spilling down his cheek. Defoe dismounted, turned him on his side, and watched his breathing. When he was certain the man lived, Defoe found himself weeping. What was wrong with him? Overcome with remorse, he retrieved the ham from his saddle bag, wrapped it in the man's hat, and left it beside him to find as a gift when he came to.

*

By five o' clock, Defoe reached Windsor just as rain fell. He passed straight through, looking for humble lodgings at a dismal village beyond, where he would not be recognised. Intermittently, throughout the journey, he found himself reciting, as if in prayer, his wife's parting words. 'I really don't know how I'd cope if something awful happened to you.'

Oxford: 'I can promise nothing.'

Chapter 5

Mr Leonard Digges attends the Ball

Beyond the gates the Queen's guests had to negotiate a path through the clutter of coaches and restless horses kicking up mud, then walk up a long staircase past double ranks of Beefeaters armed with halberds and vast hounds whose slobbering made the marble stairway treacherous. Though the guards pretended not to look – 'You're on duty!' their captain scolded – they noted a few individuals from the best families wearing authentic, ancient costumes, rescued from previously forgotten vaults by wearers whose ancestors actually were present at the court of Queen Elizabeth. One who appeared to possess such an ancient costume was the Queen's First Lady of the Bedchamber, the Duchess of Somerset, whose Percy forebears had been among England's leading families for centuries. Others, only recently elevated to greatness, had commissioned gaudy outfits from tailors who lacked original patterns on which to base them; this resulted in strange hybrids, some even combining Elizabethan ruffs and doublets with latter-day periwigs and beauty spots.

But inside the great St George's Hall none of that mattered. The groups stood clustered tightly under the bright light of hundreds of candles. Each one spilled laughter and nervous chat; swelling with new arrivals, dissolving and coming together in new formations. Here and there confident individuals trotted from group to group, becoming for a moment the laughing centre of attention. Then they glided away again, in search of greater triumph elsewhere.

Shortly after seven o' clock, a man handed his visiting card to a footman, who took it in at a glance. 'Leonard Digges,' the footman called aloud, with an admirable impersonation of enthusiasm, as though this name, the umpteenth, possessed absolutely revelatory significance.

Daniel Defoe took back the card bearing his false name. Then he stepped inside.

*

He was dark, the man who called himself Digges, though not exceptionally dark, and of middle height. He had a wide mouth and a slightly hooked nose, but otherwise looked unremarkable. Master of cosmetics, inventor of his own prosthetics, he could appear young and handsome, as he wished, or ancient and withered. Today, you'd have said he was aged somewhere around forty-five. As for his costume, it was plausibly Elizabethan, but not extravagant. Amid the outfits of the other guests at Windsor, all bright colours and dazzling brocade, he was virtually invisible – like the sort of middle-ranking functionary who would have been noticed at the court of Queen Elizabeth, if at all, only when walking backwards, cap in hand, from her presence.

That was, after all, the idea. Defoe had designed the clothes himself, with precisely that effect in mind. He'd worked for many years as a hosier, knew all about cloth, and where to get what he needed from people who were still ready to extend him credit:

imported muslins, Exeter serge, Colchester baize, Norwich crepes, silks from Spitalfields and cotton from Lancashire. Having frequently visited the homes of Britain's great men — even occasionally spending time in the royal palaces, though sometimes in awkward circumstances — he'd had the opportunity to glimpse many fine Elizabethan portraits and tapestries, committing them to memory so that he might afterwards produce a sketch. It was from just such detailed notes that he'd designed the sober costume he wore today.

*

He used the name Digges, as he had done many times previously, by way of repaying a private debt to that good religious man he'd met in the West Country. A young man, newly established as a hosier, Defoe had travelled under cover of that trade into Somerset, eventually catching up with the Duke of Monmouth's army at Sedgemoor. He met Digges, an ironmonger from Devon, on the eve of the battle. Sitting round a campfire, they pledge to fight alongside each other, and they'd done so valiantly. But travelling back to London after the failed rebellion, the two men were separated as a result of a misunderstanding — all Defoe's fault — and within less than a day he chanced to witness Digges' death. He was tarred while he still breathed, a process that produced womanish screams from his mouth and steam from his baking flesh, then hanged to rot slowly on a gibbet outside Taunton. Shortly before he expired, Digges caught Defoe's eye, then looked away. It was impossible to tell for certain if he looked away because he was in such pain, too much pain even to recognise his fellow rebel, or because he hoped by looking away to avoid casting suspicion on him. Either way, Defoe swore never to forget the man. He liked to think that by using Digges' name himself he kept his old friend alive, while the Catholic tyrant against whom they'd raised arms lay dead, far away and unburied.

The first party on this Elizabethan theme had taken place a decade ago, not long after King James's death, as it happened, though its purpose was to mark the death of Queen Anne's last surviving son. More than ever, Anne had come to identify with her Tudor predecessor, a childless woman whose dynasty ended with her. Back then, the wood-panelled audience chamber still boasted Italian tapestries, subsequently ruined by thick smoke from the new coal fires. The Queen's late husband had dressed as Elizabeth's favourite, the Earl of Essex. Today, so rumour had it, one of her privy councillors had been so bold as to assume that role. Some said it was the Lord Treasurer, Oxford; others whispered that his rival Walpole, leader of the Opposition, was the man. But this seemed unlikely: Oxford was insufficiently flamboyant to think of such a gesture, and Walpole, already firm friends with the Queen's likeliest successor, had no reason to put on such a display of affection.

For some minutes after entering the hall, Defoe stood by the door, listening to the names of other guests as they were called out no less heartily than his own had been. There were aristocrats and parliamentarians, landowners and merchants, members of the Royal Society, churchmen, physicians and diplomats, Catholics and Quakers, fops, beaux, sparks, coquettes and whores.

'Mr Joseph Addison!' the footman called. Defoe cast eyes on the writer he esteemed more than any other – the only living man whose works were assured a long posterity.

'The Duc d'Aumont!' That was the French Ambassador, whose strange expression was accounted for by a glass eye.

'Sir Alexander Spottiswode.' The Governor of Virginia.

Next came the speaker of the House of Commons, followed by the Queen's close friends, the Duke and Duchess of Somerset. The Duchess looked immaculate, her face white but for the perfect circles of crimson on her cheeks.

'The Earl of Sutherland! Mr Fentiplace Bellers!'

This was a peculiar fellow, a fop of the most absurd kind, with red heels, gemstones of all colours on his fingers and a cloud of dust that shook with every movement of his full-bottomed wig.

Defoe passed on. At the far end of the hall, by the card room, he found himself before a table covered with the greatest collection of silverware he had ever seen: plates, dishes, decanters, shakes, knives, forks and spoons. There were shoulders of lamb and great heaps of beef, cold tongue, baked woodcocks, pheasants and turkeys, delicacies such as cod's heads, great tureens of French ragouts, truffles, foods to raise the desire – such as lampreys and lobsters – white bread rolls and vast mounds of butter, basins of vermicelli, and of custard, and paper-lined boxes of sugared plums. This was the finest display of food Defoe had ever seen, by some considerable margin, and a great deal finer than the poor-man's regimen that had sustained him recently.

On one dish, the largest, lay an entire roast hog. Its back was deeply scored in a chequered pattern. This was how several people present this evening would like to see Defoe. He looked around for them, the Catholics, High Flyers, Tories, Jacobites, creditors and judicial figures before whom he had stood for sentencing. Even among the Whigs he numbered enemies.

One of them, the superlatively unpleasant Earl of Nottingham, stood only yards away. He was talking with a lanky man who wore a jester's cap. Defoe couldn't see his face, but turned away quickly.

If Nottingham saw him he was finished. It was Nottingham who had pursued Defoe a few years previously and charged him with High Crime and Misdemeanour, though he had done noth-ing to deserve it. Defoe had gone into hiding, eventually sending his wife to plead with the Earl on his behalf. This strategy pro-duced unsatisfactory results. Nottingham was not the sympathetic type: he told Sarah that Defoe must give himself up at once and in the next day's *London Gazette* advertised a £50 reward for information leading to his arrest. When Defoe was caught, at the Spitalfields home of a friendly weaver, Nottingham had him inter-rogated for two days — a substantially pointless proceeding, but painful — then sent him to Newgate Prison to serve his time in a cell with men who awaited execution. It was a horrid place: the hellish noises, the roaring and clamour, the stench and nastiness of the afflicted inmates seemed like a vision of hell — and a likely entrance to it.

Defoe knew how to affect insouciance, but even he could not pretend indifference to further stints inside Newgate. He stood motionless, eventually looking round to see that the Earl had moved away a little, though not far enough for comfort.

Defoe was intercepted by a woman dressed as a gentleman, in periwig, riding coat and sword.

'Are you alone?' she asked, without waiting for a reply. 'I have come to meet somebody, but I can't see him and I have lost my companion. Would you mind if I joined you?'

Defoe said he would be delighted, adding that his name was Digges. She introduced herself as Roger Flanders. She was already well into her late twenties, still attractive, though her bloom was fading. Her manner seemed to be that of a much younger woman.

'You are a bold man, Mr Flanders,' said Defoe. His grin dared her to admit her true name. But to do so was risky: if she were recognised she'd be called a common whore. Rather than admit she was alone, she told Defoe she had come with a married companion, a lodger with her family at Mayfair.

'For virgins, to keep chaste, must go abroad with such as are not so.' She looked at him expectantly, waiting for him to identify what he assumed must be a line from some fashionable poem. But he didn't. 'And now the silly woman has got lost.'

'Well, she can't have gone far,' he said. 'Are you from Dublin?'

'Oh, goodness,' she replied, 'do you know me?'

'My real name is Hesther Vanhomrigh,' she said

Chapter 6

The Greatest Writer in England

'I never had the pleasure of seeing you before,' Defoe said. 'Nor have I visited your native city, but I have an acute ear for accents.'

'Well, anyway, I might as well admit I gave you a false name,' she said. 'My real name is Hester Vanhomrigh. I came here to surprise a friend.'

'Delighted to make your acquaintance.' He bowed again, then asked for the name of her sweetheart.

She noted with evident pleasure his assumption that her 'friend' was her sweetheart, even allowing herself to grin. 'I hope you shan't take it badly, but if I told you his name, that would embarrass him. I can only say he's a good man, a true Christian, and a writer whose skill has been extremely useful to the Lord Treasurer. Oxford has called him the greatest writer in England.'

Defoe bridled, but gave nothing away. Indeed, he said nothing – an old trick to get additional information from people embarrassed by silence in conversation. And after a short pause, as he had expected, she continued to speak. Her sweetheart was regarded by some who knew only his writing as a cruel man, but she had seen his gentler side. Only the day before, she'd been with him at Chelsea, watching him swim in the Thames like a child, ducking beneath the surface to hide or showing only his heels for two minutes at a time. He also wrote poetry, and he wished that was as well-known as his pamphlets.

'I can honestly say,' Defoe replied, 'he sounds exactly like the kind of person I like best. And, if I might add, he's a very lucky man.'

Miss Vanhomrigh blushed. Defoe did not attempt to exploit that but changed the subject by asking if she'd been to Windsor before. She had not.

'Come with me.' She looked nervous, but he pointed to a nearby window, from where he could show her features of the castle. He needed a pretext for moving away from where they stood, becoming increasingly nervous that he might be spotted.

'Where do the servants sleep?' Miss Vanhomrigh asked. Many people would not reveal such ignorance. She evidently felt comfortable with Defoe.

'That depends. What do you mean by servants? The Arch-bishop of Canterbury has rooms of his own, which are said to be large and well furnished – though I have never seen them myself. The Lord Treasurer has the same, I'm told, as do some other great men. But the servants who squeezed the oranges and lemons in your cordial live on top of each other like common paupers. Ten to a room, or five to a cupboard. The doors that keep back these crowds are concealed all over the building, disguised amid the plasterwork and other fittings. You have only to stand in a corridor for five minutes, without making a sound, and the servants will tumble upon you from the most unexpected places.'

'I couldn't do that! They'd throw me out!'

'The servants in these places are trained above all to be polite and helpful. But if you venture too far, in my experience, they will follow you discreetly, in pretence that they must draw the curtains or poke the fire, and quietly point out your mistake.'

They spoke for several minutes more, Defoe comfortable in this teacherly manner, though he never ceased to include her in the flow of ideas and anecdote, while looking about continually for his enemies, and when prominent or exotic individuals passed by he pointed them out for her scrutiny.

'Sir Roland Gwynne.'

'The Bishop of Bristol.'

'The Lady Camarthen.' Beautiful enough in her way, brightly decked out in the feathers of parrots and peacocks, but one of those ladies who batted her fan so busily she might have been an apothecary fighting flies from a pot of treacle.

Next to pass them was the great book collector Sir Robert Cotton, whose library was said to be greater than the Lord Treasurer's. Behind Sir Robert, arriving alone, was Lady Orkney, the plain-looking former mistress of the late King William: Defoe could not help noticing that her teeth were black, and she drooled behind her fan: a sure sign that she took mercury to cure the French disease. Next: the Duke and Duchess of Richmond – recently returned, Defoe guessed, from France; Mr 'Beau' Nash, the master of ceremonies at Bath; Mr John Wilks, the comic actor; Mr Edmund Hoyle, the card player; and Mrs. Manley, the Tory satirist. An Italian castrato. A mulatto heiress from Virginia. Lt Gen Emmanuel Scroope with his wife, Ruperta, whose father was the late Prince Rupert, making her a cousin of the Queen's Protestant heir. A notable Catholic landowner, Henry Esmond, entered with Archibald Hutcheson, the Tory MP. Then the Earl of Portmore brought his wife, Catherine Sedley – formerly King

James's whore – her grown-up daughter by the old king, now Duchess of Buckingham, and two young sons by the Earl.

'How thrilling! I never saw anybody when I was a girl. Nobody interesting, I mean. That is the trouble with Ireland: there is nobody to see except the Irish.'

He had more important things to do, but the girl was charming, and she gave him a useful cover for watching others.

He asked about her family. When had they left Dublin? She told him she was the oldest daughter of a gentlewoman, and expected to inherit a great sum. She had come to England seven years ago with her mother and sister, after the death of her father. On the journey over, she'd met the man to whom she had already alluded, and with whom her entire family had forged a close friendship. It was only a matter of time, her mother firmly believed, till his great worth would be recognised by the gift of a comfortable living in the Church of England. 'And then we might marry.'

'I hope that happens soon – for his sake.'

She blushed again. Defoe wondered what could possibly make such a woman think herself bold enough to carry out her cross-dressing adventure. But it was attractive to him, this combination of boldness and innocence, and he envied the man who had won her heart.

'Oh I do hope so. In fact, I came here to press his case on the Lord Treasurer, who has it in his power to make the appointment if he wished. But I had not imagined so many others would have come to court with similar ideas.' She paused. 'Those who marry for love seem always doomed to suffer the most agonising delays, or worse. Have you noticed that?'

It seemed a good time for Defoe to excuse himself. He bowed to

Miss Vanhomrigh. She curtsied and leaned close to whisper in his ear, 'You have been very gallant.' The warmth of her breath, her handsome appearance and the generosity of her comment combined to stir something inside him. He squeezed her gloved hand and bowed again.

Wandering through the nearby gaming tables, he spied Nottingham again. He'd heard the Earl cheated at cards and his curiosity was stronger than his fear. He couldn't resist walking over to join the crowd standing by the Earl's chair, and watching him play.

In the course of his espionage, Defoe had come to believe it was possible to read a man's secret motives by close watching: everything from his fingernails (were they hard-bitten?) to his expression and his gestures gave away a man's character. Taken altogether, these signs could not fail to enlighten a curious observer. So would Defoe be able to tell if the Earl was cheating?

Daniel Defoe put on at all times an air of cheerful resolution

Chapter 7

Searching for Lady Masham

Lady Mary Arden had taken the long way through the castle hoping she might run into Samuel Holland, and she was ready to greet him with a smile that would convey exactly how happy she felt. But she had to hurry. The Queen hated to be left alone, and she was meant to be looking for Lady Masham.

The great halls were crowded to a degree Mary had never seen before. It was like Virgil's armies, in which soldiers had no room to draw their swords. At court Mary had become accustomed to the mingled odours of rank armpits, lavender water, putrid gums, the exhalation of consumptives, sweaty foodstuffs, musk and *sal volatile* − but the stench today was much worse than usual.

Every person of even the slightest consequence seemed to have come to court, but not Samuel. How was that possible? But then, if he was here she would never spot him, not unless he was stand- ing right by her, because the only thing she could see over the heads of her neighbours were the feathers in ladies' hats. She couldn't see Lady Masham either. And if she didn't get back soon she was sure Lady Masham would be back before her, and then she would be scolded again.

Beyond the thickest groups, gathered around the doors, she found that, even some distance inside, there was little in the way of open space. She wondered if anybody was going to dance at such a crowded event, and whether there were seats available for others to watch them. Certainly, she could see no dancing herself, and such music as she could hear was all but drowned out by the thunder of shouted conversation. She listened closely. It was a piece she'd played herself, often enough, from Lully's comedy-ballet, 'Le Bourgeois Gentilhomme'.

She overheard a man standing nearby say to his neighbour that the number of plain women at court was disgraceful, and out of all proportion to the country at large. 'A multitude of ugliness!' he laughed. 'This evening, thank God, the situation has improved.' He'd seen several beautiful women, including one dressed in men's clothing. Next time he saw her, he boasted, he would find some way to lure her into a corner, pull down her breeches, and . . . ! But at that point, he seemed to realise that Mary was listening, and found a more decorous way to finish what he was saying. 'I know what it is to whisper pleasant tales in a lady's ear!'

After fifteen minutes Mary grew tired of being continually pressed against by people with whom she was wholly unac-quainted. She decided to look into the card room, briefly. It was no less hot and crowded. Samuel liked to watch card games. But he was not there: the only faces she knew belonged to the Earl of Nottingham and the Duchess of Somerset, who was moving away. Mary liked the Duchess, who'd endured more than Lady Masham gave her credit for and told the story of her hardship with good humour. An only child, and last of the Percy family, the Duchess had been brought up by a grandmother who married her off, at twelve, to a boy who died shortly after. Again, her grand-mother had plans for her. And again her husband died: this one was shot dead in a duel, five bullets in the belly by a man acting on behalf of another would-be husband, eager to get his hands on the Percy fortune. Finally she had married the young Duke of Somerset, with whom she had thirteen children. Most interesting was that, after the first husband died, she'd been considered a match for the Elector of Hanover. 'Just imagine, Mary, I could have been Queen!' she once confided with a grin. 'What a lucky escape! The man is a monster, and his wife is mouldering in prison.'

Queen Anne too, as a young woman, had been matched with the German Prince. But when he came to England to propose, he changed his mind. And that was why the Queen couldn't stand to talk about him, no more than she could stand to speak about the Pretender.

Coming out of the card room, Mary found herself pulled along by a surge of sweating red faces pressing towards the tea service – so perhaps there had been dancing after all. And just at that moment she was almost knocked over by little Lord Colyear, rushing to his mother and clenching her skirts.

His mother was listening to the Duchess of Somerset, who beckoned Mary to join them without ceasing to speak. Mary modestly stepped into the group and curtsied. She watched the boy, who knew better than to interrupt. He quietly slipped his hand into his mother's and stared at the sparkling diamonds in the ring she was given, long ago, by King James. She also wore turquoise and ruby and emeralds, which Charles's father gave her when she finally married.

The Duchess stopped talking and pointed to Charles. Why was he unhappy? The boy looked to his mother for approval before daring to say anything.

'Well?' she said.

'It's nothing, Mama.'

'Come, tell us what has happened.'

The boy was struggling. His mother bent low to let him whisper in her ear. Then she laughed, stood up and said: 'It seems little Charles has been teased by some girls.'

He looked mortified, hardly believing she would betray him like that.

Buckingham said, 'What! Brought to tears by girls! Tell us what they said, little man, and we'll soon put your mind at rest.'

'They called my mother a whore,' Charles announced desperately. 'And they called me a bastard. And they said my father is an old man who looks peculiar, and they said my sister has more pride than any mercer's wife in Bedlam.'

That stopped them laughing. The boy seemed to feel further explanation was unnecessary. Mary regretted standing here to witness it.

His mother rapidly steered Charles away from the others, stopping beside Mary. Lowering herself to the boy's level, she whispered sternly, 'Charles, you are not to speak with such girls again. Who were they? Can you point them out?'

He turned towards the area he had come from. 'That's her, behind that fat man with his arms folded.'

'Do you mean Mr Walpole?'

'Yes, Mama.'

'And is that the girl – the one dressed in black velvet?'

'Yes, Mama. Her name's Sophia Howe.'

'Well, you have nothing to cry about. Sophia Howe is no better than you. In fact she's a lot worse.'

'That's what I said, Mama, for you told me that her mother is the daughter of Prince Rupert, and he's only a prince, and he never married her mother either. But she said it was better to be bastard cousin of the German Elector than bastard grandson of a Catholic king that's dead.'

Before replying, his mother glanced at Mary. It was hard to tell what the expression meant: did she regard Mary as a friend, or merely insignificant?

'Well, I'm sorry she said that, but if it's any consolation she has not got her facts right. When Mama was younger she was King James's mistress. If that makes her a whore, so be it. And if that makes your sister a bastard, so be it. But it's always better to be a king's daughter, even if your mother is not his wife, than to be the daughter of anybody else. Your half-sister Catherine is the Queen of England's half-sister. If that makes her proud – and God knows it does – who would it not? And you are the brother of the sister of the Queen, which makes you her brother too, in a manner of speaking.' She looked at Mary again, then added, 'You are hardly less her brother than James Stuart, whom we pray each night shall succeed her.'

'Am I the Pretender's brother too?' Charles asked. He must have known he was not, but seemed to find the idea enchanting.

'Not exactly, but when he sees you he will certainly love you as though you were. You must not take these taunts so painfully, dear Charles. If anybody calls you the son of a whore you must bear it, for you are so; but if they call you a bastard, fight till you die, for you are an honest man's son. Your father is a brave soldier and a loyal servant of the crown. And as I've told you before, we don't call our true king the Pretender. You never know – he might be listening.'

Charles was amazed. Did she mean the Prince was here, at

Windsor? But he knew better than to ask directly. 'I'm sorry, Mama,' he said.

The Duchess grabbed Mary's hand. 'Mary, don't wander idly. You must press through with a purposeful expression, as if searching for somebody particular. It's the only way to protect yourself from the bores who haunt the castle.' Mary smiled, and curtsied – then left the ball.

*

How suddenly the precincts of the castle emptied out. She went to a certain gallery where she had once before exchanged words with Samuel, and found him waiting for her. He was wearing a doublet and hose, and looked magnificent. They stood apart, in case anybody should see them.

'You got my poem?' he asked.

'I love it.'

'I sent another. This morning.'

'Please don't. It's too dangerous.'

Somebody was scraping along the passageway on crutches. She didn't know him personally, but recognised him at once: Alexander Pope. Since he was twelve years old the poet had been trapped in the body of a boy; people said he wore a corset beneath his tiny suit to support a spine no harder than cheese. Mary greeted him boldly: 'Good evening, Mr Pope. I hope you are well. You don't know me. My name is Mary Arden and I'm one of the Queen's ladies-in-waiting. I wanted to offer my congratulations on your "Rape of the Lock". It's wonderful, really wonderful.' She glanced at Samuel. 'I can hardly imagine that a poem could give greater pleasure.'

'You are too kind,' Pope smiled.

Mary continued: 'I read it again and again and each time I laughed. I had the honour of reading it aloud to the Queen and she enjoyed it enormously too. For my own part, though that amounts to little, I believe your poetry will endure for as long as poetry itself . . . They say you have started your version of Homer. Is that right? When can I read it?'

It was a long speech, but it spilled out easily enough because Mary meant every word.

When she'd first spoken to him, Mr Pope looked startled – he'd actually tugged at his collar, and looked about him as if to find an escape – but by the end of her speech he could hardly have shown greater satisfaction. He was young, but years of ill health had deeply lined his forehead. But now he beamed. 'You are kind. Thank you so much. Thank you. I'm sorry if I seemed unfriendly but I thought you were going to ask me to read something you had written. It was selfish. My Homer is looking for subscribers. Do you have any suggestions?' Without waiting for an answer, he added, 'And who is this?'

'My name is Holland, sir. Samuel Holland.'

Pope bowed. Mary asked if he needed help getting around the castle. Again he thanked her and said he knew his way very well. She couldn't fail to notice that Mr Pope glanced at her chest, and she felt a pang of disappointment. But he ogled furtively, not boldly, and she decided to forgive him on account of his condition.

After bowing two or three times, he set off again. She wondered where he could possibly be going.

Suddenly, Samuel said, 'I must be going. Meet me tomorrow in the rose garden – first thing!' and she was alone. But then a voice called her:

'Mary.'

'Father!'

She understood why Samuel had disappeared.

Ordinarily, Mary would have been delighted to see her father, and would have rushed over. But now she held back.

He was distracted, irritable, but he cheered up when he saw her, raising Mary from her low curtsey, taking her head in his hands and kissing her forehead gently. She hoped he would not notice that she felt nervous.

'Was that who I think it was?' he said.

'Mr Pope.'

'He's doing very well.'

'He keeps the old faith, Father.'

'No great handicap for a poet.' He paused. 'What are you doing here? Doesn't the Queen need you? And shouldn't you have somebody with you?' He'd told her often enough of the dangers facing a young woman alone; of the noblemen and baronets who delighted in forcing young ladies away to remote farmhouses, and forced marriage, or worse. He was more concerned about her than ever, because she had ceased to be the plain girl she was two years ago. At fifteen she'd been awkward, with uneven skin, lank hair and too-strong features. Now she was altogether transformed: her complexion had improved, she curled her hair, her features were softened by plumpness and colour, and her eyes sparkled with animation. She had all the accomplishments that a girl of her age and situation could possess: she could draw better than most, wrote beautiful letters crammed with insightful accounts of every new acquaintance and interesting conversation and to watch her at the harpsichord was a true pleasure. But where those had once seemed her principal merits, now they were only ornaments. She was affectionate, cheerful and open, full of lively curiosity without affectation, and no longer awkward or shy.

'She wanted to see Lady Masham,' she replied. 'We went to visit her in her rooms, but Lady Masham was not there, so Her Majesty sent me to find her. I thought best to leave the footman with Her Majesty.'

'And where is the Queen now?'

'Sleeping on Lady Masham's bed.'

Mary's father was always careful not to embarrass her by asking too much about the Queen's private matters. Nor did he press her with politics because she might feel obliged to raise matters with her royal mistress, and, by doing so, compromise her position. But he was unable to hide his surprise at what she told him. 'Gone to visit her bedchamber woman! That's quite unusual is not it? How did you get her there?'

Mary confirmed that it was unusual, and said they'd carried the Queen through the castle in a sedan chair.

'Does this mean she is feeling better? Will she be appearing at the ball?'

'Not especially better, Father. To me she seems worse than ever. A very sick woman. I'm worried for her.'

Mary's mother had died, a victim of smallpox, when Mary was eight. It would not be right to say that she looked to the Queen as a mother, but he hoped she would not lose her.

'Well, if Her Majesty is unwell you should get back to her at once. I wish I could help you find Lady Masham but I have not seen her for some time.' He kissed his daughter again on the fore-head, clasping her cheeks in his soft hands, and walked back towards the ball. Then he stopped, turned back with a puzzled frown, plunged his hand into his pocket and pulled out some papers. 'Your friend has sent another letter.'

She panicked, thinking he might have opened it and discovered her secret. But the seal was unbroken and her father gave her a smile – a little forced, perhaps, but well meant – as he handed it to her. Her secret was safe, for now anyway. As he walked away, Mary watched him go with real pain. She'd not done anything wrong, as she saw it, but felt terribly guilty all the same. Her father had taken delight in her since she was a helpless infant, encouraged and loved her through every stage of her childhood and her education to womanhood. She had never been put to any test that deserved to be called a test, so how would her dear father react when he found out that the event that should crown all his wishes was to be spoiled by her choice of husband – a man who, despite his handsome inheritance of three-thousand pounds a year, could hardly inspire more hatred from her father if he were the most unfeeling libertine.

She remembered that the letter had been sent to her father's house and the idea that he might have opened it chilled her. Why had Samuel sent it there, instead of to Windsor? More than a year had passed since she joined the Queen's staff and though they travelled constantly from palace to palace she'd been at Windsor for weeks already. Samuel must know that, since he promised to come here this evening. Had he forgotten? Was he trying to be discovered? Or did his servant make a mistake? Their families, though they felt hatred towards each other, lived in the same parish and worshipped at the same church. That was how Mary first became friends with Hannah Holland, at Sunday school. Their fathers had allowed the friendship – but only at church – because how could two little girls cause harm? And as the girls grew older they became more discreet. It was possible that the same servant who had delivered Hannah's letters while Mary still lived with her father had paid no heed to Samuel's directions and had taken this letter to her old home by force of habit. She might never find out, but sincerely hoped it would not happen again.

Shortly before Mary was born, her father had renounced his Catholic faith for the sake of the family. It would be impossible to continue living as they wished, he used to tell her, unless they publicly embraced the Church of England. It had not been an easy decision. As a Catholic, his chances of success in the world had seemed decent under King James, but afterwards they were massively reduced. But if he renounced his faith, eternal dam, nation awaited him. There was also, while he still lived in this world, the fierce disapproval of his family and friends. Mary's mother, herself from one of England's foremost Catholic families, had argued passionately against his changing religion.

Mary, who took her mother's first name but was baptised and confirmed in the Church of England, could see both sides of the argument. Restrictions on Catholics were severe after King James fled the country, as her father never ceased to remind her, and many other Catholics had done as he did. But she regretted that, as if to compensate for giving up his faith, her father had become zealously Tory. He hated Whigs with the kind of passion he would once have put into his devotions, because it was the Whigs who created the conditions that made him leave Rome.

Mary had always been sympathetic to Catholics and her father never discouraged that. On the contrary: on her tenth birthday he gave her a rosary that had once belonged to his great,grandfather. 'They are said to have been touched by the sainted Margaret

Clitherow,' he told her, referring to the butcher's wife who was stripped and pressed to death for harbouring priests in Queen Elizabeth's time. How funny to have them with her today, at this ball in honour of Elizabeth. It seemed clear that Lord Arden remained a Catholic at heart, whatever form his public devotions took.

Mr Pope had clung to the faith and seemed to enjoy great success. But he was forbidden to practise law, to own a horse or carry a gun. Worse still, Catholics couldn't live within ten miles of Hyde Park Corner, and nor could they inherit land or buildings, and it was this especially that tempted children to reject their parents' religion.

And was not that, more or less, what Mary was doing now, rejecting everything her father stood for by attaching herself to a Whig? He certainly would see it like that, when he found out, unless she could think of some way to show that Samuel's individual merits were greater than any residual qualities attaching to him as a member of the Holland family.

She sighed, and sat down on a bench overlooking the park. She took the letter from her pocket, and broke the seal to read it. It was short, and for the first time Samuel wrote directly as himself, with no attempt at concealment.

My dearest Mary

I can't wait to see you again. To be away from my betrothed, if I may call you that, is to burn in the fires of hell. Oh, Mary, I'm no writer, but that's how it feels!

I shall look for you at the ball. Please be there my love.

Samuel

Then she read the earlier letter again, drinking in every line, to learn Samuel's poem by heart. Then she folded it away, and in doing so she noticed that, while the first letter had been stamped, on the wax seal, with the image of a bird in a cage — like all the letters before it — the latest letter bore no stamped impression at all. Had Samuel forgotten? Or was it possible that Mary's inquisitive father had opened it, then resealed it? She flushed. Oh no!

But she had no time to be idle. She stood up and started to look again for Lady Masham. The Queen would be wondering where they had gone.

Nobody who met Mary could ever imagine that she would direct the course of history

Chapter 8

Those Lips! Those Eyes!

Defoe was watching Nottingham at cards. The game was *vingt-et-un*. The Earl was doing rather better than his opponents, with a large pile of gold before him. It didn't take Defoe long to work out that the Earl was reading signals from a man standing behind his opponents – a man Defoe recognised. It was the villain who had come to his house the previous evening and threatened him. He was considerably more than six feet tall, his complexion waxy, his left cheek disfigured by a livid scar running from his eye to his chin, a grim appearance only partially offset by his costume of Elizabethan court jester, complete with bells on his cap.

Each player put forward five sovereigns before the banker dealt the first card, face down. Then they looked at the card and placed another bet.

Nottingham's man, who loomed above the rest of the onlookers opposite, had a clear view of the other players' cards. Defoe watched the man carefully and soon made sense of the signals: a scratch of the nose encouraged Nottingham to bet high, whereas a fidget with the waistcoat told him not to bet any more on this hand.

He had not intended to stay long, and waited only to watch

Nottingham win the next hand. Two other players had burst, and the last showed nineteen. Nottingham placed his cards down: a ten followed by a jack. In that hand alone, Nottingham won more money than Defoe owed when Nottingham had refused to let his debts be discharged.

All of a sudden, Defoe became aware that the Earl's man had noticed him. He must move away at once.

Returning to the tables of food, and helping himself to a leg of turkey in honey, he cursed himself for making such a blunder. He had not eaten for some time and took a small bite from the glisten/ ing drumstick: it was tough meat, but delicious. He could have eaten ten of them. Then he turned to glance casually at the card tables. The Earl's man had left the game and was walking out of the card room towards him.

Disaster! The Earl would never forgive it him if he knew Defoe had seen how he cheated. But perhaps the man had not recognised him. Perhaps he was following simply because he was hungry. Still holding the turkey in a linen napkin, Defoe moved away from the food tables, walking as quickly as possible without attracting the attention of onlookers. Head towards the far end of the room, he thought. Through the doorway into the next hall. From there, through the dense crowd to an exit.

He found himself at the foot of two magnificent staircases. There was nobody about. Looking back into the hall he saw the jester's cap bobbing above the crowd towards him. Still coming! Defoe turned towards the stairs and ran up to a landing, almost knocking over a man he would later identify as Dr Arbuthnot. Then he saw another man, who glanced briefly at Defoe as he entered a room further along the corridor. Defoe recognised him at once. The Pretender! Of all the times to see him! There was nothing to be done. He'd have to lose Nottingham's man and come back. On instinct, he dashed down the stairs again and curled up as small as he could manage in a cubbyhole hidden among the plasterwork. Breathe slowly, he told himself. Don't panic. And get rid of the turkey. He took another bite of the drumstick and shoved the rest, wrapped loosely in the napkin, into one of his pockets, then slipped the silk scarf from his neck, wrapping the ends tightly around each hand in readiness to throttle anyone who might come for him.

For several moments there was no sound. Perhaps the man had not seen him come this way after all. But just as he started to loosen the scarf he heard a noise that stopped his breath: the man's footsteps moved steadily over the marble towards him, drawing nearer and nearer. This was it! He heard the man's breathing, and a muttering of curses. He obviously couldn't decide where to look next. Then the footsteps moved on to the stairs above Defoe's head and he heard the crash of a door being slammed open. The footsteps recommenced, and to Defoe's indescribable joy and gratitude they died slowly away again till they could be heard no more. It was a miracle. But if God had allowed him to escape he must not take that divine mercy for granted. He repented his arrogance and determined to concentrate fully on the task at hand.

All the same, he waited several minutes more before daring to move. He'd been a fool, risking the entire mission out of idle curiosity. The man was sure to come back and keep looking for him, but there was work still to be done. He thought of the face he had seen before: those unmistakable lips. And the eyes! Despite looking furtive, the Pretender positively believed his life's ambition was within his grasp. The Queen was in no state to deal with such a man, to judge by all Defoe had heard. He must go back upstairs

71

and find the Pretender as soon as the way was clear. He would have to think carefully about what to do when he found him – kill him? The Pretender's supporters would not allow it without a fight. Even the Queen, though she denied the Pretender was her brother, might object to him being killed at her fancy-dress ball. Anyway, how to do it? Shoot him? Too noisy. Drop arsenic in his food? Not much use if he was not eating. Sprinkle it over his clothes? Easier said than done. Anyway, those were the methods of a coward. Could Defoe challenge him to a duel – or provoke the Pretender into challenging him? Devising a suitable insult was hardly a problem, but the Pretender probably didn't fight his own duels. He'd have supporters to do that on his behalf. And they would be better swordsmen than Defoe.

The best thing was to see what happened. Rather than tie himself up with a predetermined plan, he would wait for the opportunity, then improvise. The mission was more dangerous than ever, but he still felt it was within his abilities. One thing seemed clear, though: if Nottingham's man reappeared, Defoe would have to kill him, too.

*

He returned to the ballroom, and started talking to the first man he could find alone. Sir Roderick Whitehouse took a snuffbox from his pocket and snorted a copious pinch of Spanish before asking, 'Do you think the Queen will appear tonight, Mr Digges?'

He was a Tory baronet from the West Country. Defoe knew the type: a man with a thousand acres, devoted only to his dog and his gun. He looked ill at ease in his costume, like some village butcher dressed up as Sir Thomas More, and every so often scratched violently at the skin beneath his squashy hat.

Defoe replied cautiously, 'We must have faith in the Queen's physician.'

'I would not be so sure, Mr Digges. I was speaking just now to a man who had talked earlier with Dr Arbuthnot, and he said you could count the remainder of her life in days, not weeks.'

Defoe's mind raced. A man by the name of Arbuthnot had written the *History of John Bull*; a decent piece of satire, although designed to help the Tories to end the war with France. The author's brother, he seemed to recall, was agent to the Pretender in France. What if this doctor was himself in the pay of the Pretender – even now poisoning the Queen to smooth the way for the papist impostor? That was quite possible. Defoe remembered reading of a similar plot against Queen Elizabeth by her doctor, the Catholic Jew from Spain, Ruy Lopez.

Sir Roderick offered a piece of advice. 'This ball is the best opportunity you will find, Mr Digges, to make friends to see you through the upheavals of the succession.'

Few people could concentrate for even a short time on anything else; it seemed that everybody was writing letters to men of influence, or actually visiting court to buttonhole them personally. That seemed to be the case with this baronet. 'I managed to have a word with the Chancellor yesterday,' he whispered. 'I knew he could do nothing for me himself but he was not altogether discouraging. Gave me the name of a gentleman in the Southern Department who is entering my name on a special file. Something may come of it.'

Defoe smiled. It remained unclear whether the man favoured the Protestant succession or the return of the Pretender. Glancing over the baronet's shoulder in the look-out for Nottingham's man, Defoe caught the eye of a girl of fourteen or so, standing nearby. She looked bored, evidently unwilling to conceal it. Defoe bowed to her. Sir Roderick, looking round, did the same. Before responding, the girl glanced towards a woman whom Defoe took to be her mother, but the woman was otherwise occupied so the girl, deciding it could do no harm to speak with them so long as she didn't move, said her name was Sophia Howe. She was from Norfolk, and had come to court with her mother and grandmother.

'And that is my grandmamma,' she added, as though this were some great worthy. The two men turned to look. But all three quickly looked away again: the ancient woman, believing herself to be unobserved, was taking the opportunity to adjust the plumpers that filled out her cheeks.

Sophia covered up this embarrassment by stating frankly that she loved her grandmother. But like all ancient people, she conjectured, Mrs Hughes didn't belong to the present. She dragged herself to balls and sat in a corner, dressed in the fashions of the last century and nobody took any notice of her, particularly not now her best friend Mrs Barry was dead. Mrs Barry had been an actress, like Grandmamma, and died last year of a bite from her rabid lapdog. Everybody was very sorry, Sophie said. Grandmamma had been left a great sum of money by Mama's father, Prince Rupert, but she had gambled it all away and now the family was poor. Mama wished that the new king, when he arrived, might appoint Sophia lady-in-waiting to the queen, but Sophia couldn't see how it helped to stand here smiling at a lot of insignificant people.

She wore a dress of black velvet and a petticoat of flame-coloured brocade. A sapphire bodkin sparkled in her hair, prettily displayed in fashionable curls about the neck and temple. In her hand she carried a half-mask to hide her eyes, but she'd evidently decided not to use it. What was the point? And what was the point of coming to court at all, and all those lessons she'd learned with her dancing master, learning to present herself correctly, if the Queen would never appear?

'Is the Duke of Marlborough here?' she asked. 'And the Duchess?'

Defoe knew enough of the hatred between the Queen and her former favourites to say only that he had not seen them.

At that moment, a disturbance near the front door drew their attention to the arrival of the Lord Treasurer, the Earl of Oxford. A group of his supporters politely applauded. Men and women standing nearby bowed and curtseyed. All round the room, heads turned to stare. Oxford's response was to smile back with an expression of the utmost humility.

'Forget the Duke of Marlborough, my dear,' the baronet said. 'That is the most important man in Great Britain.' After a long pause, he added: 'But for how long? For weeks, or only days?'

Sophia said: 'But if you spoke to Oxford he might invite you to his levee . . .'

'What do I want to do that for?' laughed Sir Roderick, affronted that a mere girl should make so bold as to offer advice. 'To stand humbly by while he shaves, and jostle with hundreds of others for a few minutes of private *tete-a-tete*? I should be obliged to fawn in a manner I couldn't bear, for you know well that powerful men are always the better jesters. I should be like a broker, always ready to laugh with a merchant even when the abuse concerns himself.'

There was further commotion from the entrance. 'Look!' said

a voice nearby. Walpole stood at the top of the stairs and bowed
– and it seemed as if the whole room bowed back. Defoe instinctively looked towards Oxford. The Lord Treasurer was visibly
shocked by how enthusiastically his political opponent was
greeted, but affected unsuccessfully not to have seen by taking a
snuffbox from his pocket and helping himself to a mighty pinch
of Orangeree. Defoe felt something he'd never felt before: pity for
his patron. What do they see in Walpole? Only two years ago the
man was imprisoned in the Tower for financial mismanagement.
Now even Tories bowed deeply before him. But that would not
last long. Not if Oxford could prevent it – and not if Defoe could
help him.

At that moment, he caught sight of somebody, a tall figure,
with a jester's cap and a scar running from his eye to his chin,
pressing towards them through the crowded hall. Defoe – or
Digges – immediately took his leave.

In the hallway, he opened a door that led on to the gardens.
There was nowhere to hide. He stepped back inside and waited
for Nottingham's man to catch up with him.

'You're looking for me, sir?'

The man grinned, cleared the hilt of his sword and loosened
the blade in its sheath in a gesture of calculated menace. He's got
me this time, Defoe thought, standing motionless as the brute
strode towards him, jester's cap jingling with each step.

'You must come with me.'

The Earl of Nottingham would never forgive Defoe

Chapter 9

Doubloons, Guineas and
Pieces of Eight

Defoe guessed the man had been instructed to kill him if nec-essary but that Nottingham would prefer to question him first. That gave some comfort. What's more, though the man's scar was impressive, he did not look like much of a fighter. He was tall, but lacked bulk. Defoe decided to bluff. In a steady tone he replied, 'You dare to draw in the precincts of the castle? Treason! Put your sword away this instant, or else I promise, on my honour, you will hang at the next assizes.'

It was not the kind of speech the man expected. An expression of uncertainly passed across his face. Then a battle of looks took place between them. Finally the man put up his weapon. 'Have it your way,' he said. But he was not finished with Defoe. He grasped his arm violently. Defoe was taken by surprise, and tried to withdraw, but the man had a grip of iron. He pulled Defoe close with a single motion. 'Like it or not, you're coming with me. Don't struggle or I'll break your arm.' As he said that, he gave it a wrench and Defoe cried out despite himself.

'You can't kill me here. And you can't take me back inside. People would ask questions. I'd be obliged to reveal the secrets of the Earl's success at cards.'

78

'You shan't have the chance. We're going to the Earl's rooms.' The man nodded towards a door that led to a long passageway. When they'd gone through there, he shoved Defoe towards a pair of staircases like the one Defoe had hidden beneath earlier.

At that moment, a footman appeared above them, holding a chamber pot. Looking back on the incident, Defoe would remember him clearly, because for some reason this footman did not wear a hat, and his fine blond hair flapped around his head with each step. Nottingham's man released his grip on Defoe. What happened next was driven by instinct. Defoe suddenly remembered the cold turkey leg in his pocket. He pulled it out and waved it at the servant. 'Where can I get rid of this?'

'Allow me to take it for you,' the servant replied, coming towards them.

It was now or never. Defoe dashed to one side, in a last attempt to escape. With an explosion of oaths, Nottingham's man drew his sword and slashed violently at the air before him. Defoe felt the whoosh of air: if the sword had been an inch longer it would have split him from crown to belly.

As the sword's point hit the floor, Defoe swung his arm back and swivelled powerfully, smashing his fist into the face of his would-be captor. The blow had an upward motion and his fist still held the cold turkey: the thin end of the drumstick seemed to catch on the inside of the man's nostril, but overcame that minor obstacle, slipped along the side of the nose and then – with a noise like a spoon withdrawing from jelly – the bone penetrated the man's eye socket. At the same time, Defoe's fist, wrapped tightly around the other end of the drumstick, thumped into the base of his nose. With a crack, the man's septum crashed upwards into his brain.

This was not one of the techniques Defoe had learned from his mercenary friends, but a clenched fist, pushed up with enough force at the bottom of a man's nose was enough to do the job.

It was extraordinary, the difference between a living body and a body from which the soul has departed. Now there is someone, now there is no one. Just a while ago, this corpse had been cheating at cards. Defoe was powerfully moved by what he had done: killed a man, after all those times he'd managed to avoid it. And the mess – just look at it! The man's eye socket oozed vilely – could make a man sick if he allowed it. This incident certainly would not make the job of killing the Pretender any easier, if Defoe still got the chance. To break the Commandment at all, even when the consequence justified it, was a terrible thing. And this man's death was not strictly necessary.

Defoe thought he might be sick, but there was no time to waste. He had to be strong. The footman still stood at the bottom of the stairs, astonished, clutching the chamber pot with white knuckles. With immense regret, Defoe realised that he would have to get rid of this man too. Something of this resolve showed itself in his expression, and then the footman did something that saved his life: he fainted. The chamber pot fell to the floor, smashing into many pieces and releasing a quantity of piss that ran slowly towards the bleeding head of the dead man.

So much for Defoe's belief that he could kill cleanly.

But if this was inconvenient, it was better than having to kill the footman. With fresh resolve, Defoe rubbed his aching fist and wondered how long he had. He must at least attempt to tidy up, put the bodies somewhere they would not be found till after he'd left the castle, perhaps even returned to London. Killing a man in the castle was treason, and if Defoe was caught he'd hang. If he

tried to tell the truth, nobody would believe him. He was an out-
sider, with previous convictions and a known grudge against the
Earl of Nottingham. Nobody would come forward to swear to his
good character. If he said he was working for the Lord Treasurer,
Oxford would deny it.

Tearing the collar from Nottingham's man to stuff it in the
footman's mouth, he noticed his assailant was still breathing. Not
a murderer at all! Defoe fell to his feet and thanked his Redeemer.
But the elation was short-lived. If the man was not dead yet, he
was not going to last much longer, and Defoe could hardly fetch
him a doctor. He wondered if he should finish him off but was
not sufficiently cold-blooded to do that. There has been enough
bloodshed already.

He dragged both bodies under the stairs, in case somebody
should pass by, and after first removing the footman's shirt, with
which to mop the floor, he bound their hands and feet. Then he
checked the pockets. The footman carried nothing but a thimble,
a reel of strong thread, and a few inches of beeswax candle, stolen
presumably from a fixture in the castle. As the son of a chandler,
Defoe knew well enough how valuable it was. Nottingham's man
carried coins from several countries – doubloons, and louis-d'ors,
and guineas and pieces of eight – a key, a filthy handkerchief, a
lock of hair much fairer than his own, three sticks of tobacco and
a woman's tweezers. In his back pocket, Defoe was astonished and
dismayed to find that the man who had been waving his sword
so furiously carried a copy of Nelson's *Guide to the Festivals and
the Fasts of the Church of England*. It was inscribed to 'Darling
William' by his mother.

'God have mercy on you,' Defoe muttered, stuffing the book

along with the rest inside his own pockets. Then he went looking for a better place to hide the bodies.

When that was accomplished, he sat on the stairs twisting his cap in his hands. Instinct told him to flee the castle at once. But that seemed wrong. He'd come here ready to break the command, ments by killing a man, and he'd actually glimpsed the man in question – he was certain of it. Without a doubt, the Pretender was plotting to take the throne, and if he succeeded in that, the consequences for Defoe's people, from the humblest weaver to the Lord Treasurer himself, would be catastrophic. Oxford's instructions, unspecific though they had been, remained within Defoe's means, and if he prevented the Pretender, he might just be forgiven this man's death. Might even be hailed as a national hero, like the Duke of Marlborough after Blenheim. But if he ran away, he would have achieved nothing, except a murder that would weigh eternally on his soul.

He remembered what the baronet had told him of the Queen's physician – perhaps Arbuthnot was hiding the Pretender? With these thoughts foremost in his mind, Defoe set off in search of the doctor's rooms.

Chapter 10

A Kiss Would Be a Start

After half an hour away from the Queen, Mary was starting to panic. Where was Lady Masham? She turned the corner into a quiet gallery and heard a voice she recognised.

'Come here and kiss me,' said Bolingbroke. Mary crept closer. He was sitting on a bench in a quiet gallery still dressed up as an Elizabethan nobleman and speaking to Lady Masham. Lady Masham stood by the window fidgeting with her rings. How embarrassing! Mary could hardly intrude now, so she stood still, out of sight, and waited for a better moment.

Lady Masham ignored His Lordship's request. She had a preoccupied expression on her face. Her nose was a little long, the mouth too wide to be described as a perfect rosebud, and at thirty-five she had to be considered old – but she was attractive for her age. Bolingbroke was the father of her youngest child: they'd been lovers for two years, in which time she'd given birth to her sixth, a daughter, and come to see for herself that a mistress's life can be as painful as any wife's – she told Mary – because her man will also drink and stay out late whoring. But the Queen knew nothing of this.

Bolingbroke broke the silence again. 'The Duke of Marlborough told me a funny thing about this gallery . . .' Lady Masham gave no response, but he carried on,

'He said he was walking alone here, not long after old King Charles died, when he turned the corner and found one of the privy councillors buggering his pageboy.'

Still Lady Masham said nothing. He continued.

'It's hard to imagine now, the court being so stale these days, but back then that sort of activity went on a lot. Marlborough was a young man at that time, hardly more than a pageboy himself. Not senior enough, at any rate, to make his presence felt in such embarrassing circumstances, far less to break up the happy couple.'

Lady Masham continued to look out of the window. It was dark outside, but for the dim light of the moon on Windsor Forest.

Like his father before him, Bolingbroke was a notorious rake, commonly given to this kind of talk. The Duchess of Somerset told Mary that his mother, a daughter of the Earl of Warwick, might have exerted a more delicate influence but she died when he was a little boy. As plain Harry St John he'd married a woman who brought him a considerable fortune, but she bored him and he treated her with indifference, and even among his friends she was known as 'poor Mrs St. John'. In Paris, while negotiating for peace, he had taken for his mistress a Madame de Ferriol and also her sister Madame de Tencin. He went with one to the theatre, where the audience – conscious that their great nation could no longer afford to conduct extravagant warfare – rose to applaud the bringer of peace; with the other sister he attended an opera in the presence of the Pretender. Back in London, His Lordship was distrusted for his love of the French, he was said to have negotiated peace with the enemy and imposed it on his allies, rather than the other way round. He stooped to take English mistresses, too, including Lady Masham, and some said he ran after street whores and barmaids. The ladies at court gradually allowed these details to be known to the Queen. She disapproved: 'He is not so regular in his private life as he ought to be,' she used to say.

The Queen additionally suspected that her secretary of state was not devout. He was careless about observing even rudimen-tary forms of piety, and told Lady Masham — who repeated it to Mary — that a pious man was somebody who would be an atheist if only the Queen were. His offences were not restricted merely to negligent religious observance and roguish speech. His Lordship was once seen running naked with friends, late at night, through St James's Park. This did nothing to help his reputation with the Queen, though it hardly affected his stamina; at thirty-six, he was young enough to sustain such behaviour without any harm to his work: even after drinking till the small hours, Bolingbroke summoned people to meetings before they had time to shave. In parliament, he spoke with unmatched eloquence, in council addressed the Queen more boldly than anybody else, and among friends he swore terribly. 'My habits at court have neither taught me to show what I do not feel nor to hide what I do,' he once told the Queen. 'My love and hate are so far from not appearing in my words and actions that they generally sit in my face.' But friends who believed this, supposing him ill-suited to equivocation, often found in the long run that they were mistaken. Or so Mary's father told her.

He went on with his story. 'This put the Duke in a difficult position. Not only awkward in itself, to witness such goings on, but especially awkward because the new King, on succeeding to the throne, had specifically instructed him to put an end to that sort of thing if he came across it. Odd though it seems, the King formally announced on his accession, only minutes after he was anointed, that "Italian practices" of that sort had to end. He'd been getting complaints from the pageboys, he said – rather to the horror of the Archbishop of Canterbury. Well, the page in this instance looked perfectly happy, so rather than get involved in what didn't concern him, Marlborough decided to disappear back to wherever he'd come from.'

'Is that it?'

'No, no. Wait a moment. Because on turning the corner he bumped into the King. He had to think fast, because if the King had walked any further and seen what was going on it would have been pretty clear that Marlborough had seen it too and ignored his clear instructions.'

'What did he do?'

'Well, the King never was an easy man to steer off his predetermined course, as history has shown. But some things were guaranteed to catch his attention. The best, Marlborough told me, was to claim possession of news relating to any kind of plot against Catholics. So the Duke told His Majesty he'd been looking for him in order to pass on exactly that kind of worrying information.'

Lady Masham snorted. 'And is that what you have just done? Dragged me here on a pretext of urgent business, only to ask for a kiss?'

Mary flushed, ashamed of herself for snooping. It soon got worse.

'Of course not. But a kiss would be nice. It would be a start. I'd rather fuck, but you've not seemed especially willing, recently, in that regard. When we're in company, by all means look grave as a nun — but when we're alone you should be like a strumpet. You used to be an errant Miss Romps . . . what's the matter?'

Lady Masham ignored the question. 'You told me we needed to speak in private about something important. I have urgent enough matters to deal with of my own. The Queen is probably calling for me . . .'

'Well, fucking is important to me, but I'll let that pass . . . The fact is that Parliament has launched an investigation into the com-mercial arrangements stemming from last year's peace. The treaty, you might recall, included financial arrangements relating to the slave trade that benefited not only the Queen personally but also, on terms less publicly available, me and you. The investigation's been launched by Oxford. He's done it as a kind of revenge. I suppose I brought it on myself.'

Mary was shocked. As a lady-in-waiting, often present at the Queen's side during meetings of the Cabinet, she had become accustomed to the way politicians spoke to one another in private. But she'd never heard such transparent admissions of self-interest.

Lady Masham still faced away from him but now she turned round. 'Of course it's your fault,' she hissed. 'It's because of your stupid attack on the Dissenters. If you had not tried to embarrass Oxford by making him choose between voting for the interests of his family and the interests of his Tory supporters, he would not have launched this investigation. He knew you would be embarrassed if the peace terms became public.

'And the point is,' she continued, 'you have not brought this on yourself alone. Does Oxford not realise this will embarrass others beside you? Does he know that I will come under scrutiny? After everything I have done for him? What kind of cousin is he? I came to court with no friends when my father died, and Oxford did nothing for me. He only showed interest after the Duchess of Marlborough took an interest in me. Since I replaced her in the Queen's affections he has tried to make up for what he failed to do before. I have tried to help him when I can. But no more. Not after this.'

Lady Masham's husband, the eighth son of a baronet, was a man elevated to the peerage as one of a batch of Tories, including Bolingbroke. Bolingbroke resented his promotion – he felt he should be Earl, not merely Viscount – and Lady Masham resented her husband's promotion because it had been arranged with one humbling condition: that she continue to carry out the duties of lady-in-waiting. Thus, though everybody in Britain knew the Queen was ill, Abigail was one of the few who knew how bad things really were, witnessing the unguarded private moments, the pain and indignity concealed even from friends.

That being said, Lady Masham's position produced real benefits. Mary had seen too often that the Queen was unwilling to say no to a woman who dealt with her most intimate difficulties while also mixing with the peerage. Lady Masham once procured a regiment for her brother, Jack, against the wishes of the Duke of Marlborough. A few Whigs raised questions against it in Parliament, demanding that the Queen remove Lady Masham from service. But the Queen declined to be imposed upon.

Mary had never spoken to anybody about Lady Masham's scheming. Not with her father, nor with Samuel. Both respected her position, and the Queen's privacy, too much to inquire. But she felt increasingly burdened by what she saw. If the truth were uncovered, people might blame her for failing to say anything earlier. But who could she tell? The Duchess? Why should they believe her word against Lady Masham's? The consequences of speaking out were impossible to guess, but Lady Masham could certainly make life difficult for Mary's father, if she wished, and for Samuel, too.

'I have been looking through the Queen's private papers,' said Lady Masham.

Bolingbroke looked up, rose from his bench and walked towards her. 'Which papers do you mean?'

Mary felt faint. Breathing never was easy in a corset; now she felt she might burst. Even the strongest woman might faint in such conditions. But if she fainted they would know for certain that she'd heard them.

'She has a packet she carries with her from palace to palace, in a locked box. Yesterday I managed to look inside. There were several bundles wrapped together. I didn't get a chance to read them all but the first contained some rather hateful letters from the Duchess of Marlborough. These confirmed what I had always suspected – that after putting me in this position and seeing how much the Queen liked me, the Duchess conducted a fierce cam-paign to get rid of me. Look at this.' She pulled a pocket from under her skirt, where it hung from a ribbon round her waist, and extracted from it a piece of paper.

'You took it away!' Bolingbroke looked shocked

Mary shivered. If Lady Masham found out she had been listen-ing . . . well, Mary had no idea what she would do. Her arms and neck had gone cold, her palms were sweating. She reached for her smelling salts but remembered, just in time, that even a smell could give her away.

'Don't worry,' Lady Masham said, 'it's a copy. The original was folded inside the Duchess's letter, and that's where it is now.'

It was a piece of verse. Bolingbroke read it aloud.

'When as Queen Anne of great Renown
Great Britain's Scepter sway'd,
Beside the Church she dearly loved
A dirty Chambermaid.

'Is that supposed to be you?' Bolingbroke smiled — which made
Mary smile too. 'Ah yes. See how the next verse begins . . .

O! Lady Masham that was her Name
She stitched and starched full well,
But how she pierced this Royal Heart
No Mortal Man can tell.'

Bolingbroke paused. He said nothing this time but gave Lady
Masham another teasing look, then resumed.

'However, for sweet service done
And causes of great Weight
Her Royal Mistress made her, oh!
A Minister of State.
Her Secretary she was not
Because she could not write
But had the Conduct and the Care
Of some dark Deeds at Night.

Bolingbroke handed the paper back. He smirked.
'Don't laugh. It's true. The work I do is loathsome. It's distinctly at odds with my position.'

Bolingbroke still looked amused, but what Lady Masham said next stopped that.

'I have started to compensate myself by withdrawing sums from the Queen's bank account.'

Bolingbroke stared at her, and then grabbed her arm to pull her towards him. On instinct, Lady Masham lifted her hands to ward off a blow. None came.

'Is that my punishment for not fucking?'

Though shocked by his strength of feeling, she affected indifference. 'What is money to a sick old woman? The Queen has no remaining relatives, she's of no use to anybody – in fact a great inconvenience to those around her . . . She is certain to die soon and doesn't even know herself why she is still alive. If she were healthier, then the people who serve her could rest secure in their employments, without worrying about what will happen to them after she is gone.'

Bolingbroke was still gripping her arm. He began to ask how much she had taken when suddenly a man turned the corner and walked towards them, seemingly lost and evidently drunk. He sobered a little when he recognised the great minister of state, who released Lady Masham. 'Excuse me, my Lord, I seem to have taken a wrong turning . . . Madam, goodnight.' The man stumbled off in the direction from which he had come. After several moments of silence, Lady Masham asked: 'Do you think he heard us?'

'No, I do not. If I did I would have have knocked his brains out. What is the answer? How long have you been stealing this money, you fool?'

'I started a few weeks ago. At first I felt nervous but I soon got used to it. So far I have taken twenty thousand pounds.' As she said it, Lady Masham stared boldly into his eyes and Mary knew she must have taken even more. But Bolingbroke said nothing, so Lady Masham added: 'The Queen has no idea.'

'Why not just ask her for the money instead of stealing it? Treat her with kindness and she will do anything for you. The poor woman just wants somebody to talk to. She's always given you whatever you need.'

'She's never given me twenty thousand! And it's not stealing. It's payment. I was right to take it because among her papers I also found a new will, of recent date but still unsigned, leaving a small sum to the poor and dividing the jewellery between the Duchess of Somerset, who never lifted a finger to help her, and the last remaining relative she doesn't either loathe or refuse to recognise, the ancient Duchess of Savoy.' After a pause, she added: 'There was nothing for me.'

'Did she promise to leave you anything?'

'No. And as I said, the will was unsigned. I have no idea what the terms of any previous document might have been. But I shall do my best to keep it unsigned. That way, even if I receive nothing myself, I can at least hope the Duchess of Somerset will get nothing too.'

She paused and he frowned.

'What is the matter now?'

'Did the will mention the Pretender?' he asked. But he didn't get an answer because Mary was unable to stand still any longer. The sound of creaking floorboards gave her away.

'I'm sorry if I startled you,' she said, stepping into view. Her legs were shaking with cramp and fear, but she hoped they would not notice in the dim light. 'I wanted to warn you that Her Majesty has come to visit you.'

92

Lady Masham appeared unrattled by Mary's appearance, as if she had been discussing nothing more important than a pair of red-heeled shoes or a trip to see the lions at the Tower. 'Thank you, Mary. Where is she now?'

'I left her asleep on your bed.'

Bolingbroke's response was less carefree. Hitherto, he'd shown Mary only the interest of a gardener watching a promising flower come into bloom. Now he spoke coldly. 'You shouldn't creep up on people. How long have you been standing there?'

Lady Masham had found that a mistress's life can be as painful as any wife's

Chapter 11

A Spy Inside the Wardrobe

Defoe was taking a risk by wandering round the castle but he knew that, in some of the Queen's palaces, vagrants were said to set up home in quiet corners and live undisturbed for weeks — only being thrown out when her bodyguard took it in mind to hunt them down with her spaniels, for sport.

He was most likely to attract suspicion if he wandered aimlessly. The solution was actively to seek help from the people who might otherwise suspect him. He went looking for a footman, introduced himself and asked for directions to Dr Arbuthnot's rooms. These were promptly and politely supplied.

Shortly after, he found himself near a suite of rooms. On the doors, brass plates showed the names of various ladies-in-waiting. Servants went in and out without ceremony, carrying in fresh linen and candles and taking away dirty dishes.

Defoe took a couple of guineas from his pocket — the last money he had — and waited till a footman passed who was about the same size as him.

'Come here,' Defoe whispered with a friendly expression. 'I've a favour to ask you.'

The man looked puzzled, but smiled and asked how he could help.

'If you lend me your clothes for ten minutes, I'll give you these.' He held out the coins.

'I'm not sure . . .'

'You look like a man who would understand. Does it help if I say there is a lady involved?'

This may not have been enough to persuade him. The fellow grinned.

'Give me two guineas and I'll help you. But only for five minutes, or I'll be missed.'

Two guineas! Defoe gave him one now, and promised the other when he returned – he had no intention of returning.

'We should be all right in here,' the man said, and they went into one of the nearest suites. It was smaller than he'd imagined, but cheerfully decorated. There were flowers on the tables, and a Bible, and a doll sat up on the bed. The man wished him luck as he adjusted his clothes on Defoe. He would wait inside the privy in case another servant happened to come in. 'And please don't be more than five minutes, sir!'

When the man had hidden, Defoe pulled his paper, his pistol, the jar of arsenic, the book of prayers and the jester's hat from his greatcoat and shoved them inside his breeches. The metal felt cold on his leg. Wandering down the corridor in the servant's black livery and ill-fitting shoes, Defoe couldn't help smiling as he imagined the man sitting on the privy. One of the ladies-in-waiting would certainly have a shock when she got back. Less amusing was the idea that the man would be another witness to identify him, if word got out about the man who was most probably dead by now. With a bit of luck, the fellow would be too ashamed to come forward. Then again, he could always pretend he changed clothes unwillingly. How stupid not to have taken clothes off the fellow who fainted, instead of wiping the floor with them. But there was no point regretting what was already done. In the meantime, Defoe would be harder to find among the hundreds of servants dressed the same way.

Having negotiated his way through a series of increasingly narrow and gloomy stairways and corridors, he found himself outside Dr. Arbuthnot's door.

He waited till he was sure the passage was empty, then knocked. No answer. He knocked again, louder this time, and after a pause he tried the handle.

He stood inside a lobby, which gave on to two doors. The first led to what he guessed by the stench to be the doctor's privy. He could use that himself: his bladder was bursting in these too-tight breeches, but he had not the time to waste. The other door led to a salon with a dining table and twelve chairs. On the table stood two silver candlesticks with fresh candles. They had not been burning long, he guessed, which meant the owner of the rooms was not far away – or his servants weren't – and would return shortly. By the dim light he was unable to see to the furthest end of the room, but noted several other objects on the table: unfamiliar tools in iron, and four glass vessels. To the left, a fire was burning low before a pair of high-backed chairs. To the right, behind more chairs, stood a massive cupboard. This Defoe walked past, carrying the candles carefully, to reach the far end of the room. There he found another door and a bureau standing beneath a shuttered window. On top of the bureau lay a mess of papers. He could examine those later. First, he cautiously put down the candles on a chair and tried the drawers. The top one was locked. He must take his time, not rush himself. He tried a second, but that was locked too, and with the third and fourth he had no more success. What could they hold?

Still shaken by what he had done earlier, Defoe was in a state of extreme nervousness. The fall of coals in the fireplace, and the ticking of the clock, filled him with alarm.

He wondered if there might be some secret compartment, or a latch that released the drawers all at once. But he couldn't find it, so instead he looked through the papers arranged on top. The first sheet revealed itself to be rough notes towards a verse satire on death by consumption. There were lines drawn here and there at the bottom of the page, such as a man might make out of idleness or to test his quill. Beneath that was a list of herbs – marjoram, bracken, thyme, honeysuckle, henbane – together with the dates and duration of forced bleeding. Then a table for reducing English, French and Spanish money to a common value. What did Dr Arbuthnot need that for? Next, a letter signed by the Catholic poet, Pope, about whom Defoe already entertained suspicions. And beneath that, something that immediately grabbed Defoe's attention – and seemed to confirm his earlier conjecture – a letter from Dr Arbuthnot's brother, sent from the Pretender's court in exile at St Germain in Paris. But he had hardly started to read it when he heard footsteps outside. This time there could be no mistake. He had to decide at once whether to hide, or to show himself and invent some story. On an instinct that he was later to regret immensely, he decided to hide. Hurriedly stuffing both letters inside his doublet, he grabbed the candles, spilling wax on the floor, and dashed back through the room. He placed the lights more or less where they had stood previously and stepped inside the tall cupboard. He was unable to see what was inside, but pushed in and created a space for himself. As he did so, something rattled. He stuck out a hand to still it in the darkness, but the thing was longer than he expected, reaching from the height of his head to the floor. It comprised odd pieces, textured like wood or rough stone, each one attached to the other by tiny wires. He ran his fingers up from the bottom, pausing to feel carefully the topmost part: it was round, and smooth, and on its front he was able to sink his fingers into a pair of large cavities. With a shock he suddenly realised his fingers were resting inside the eye sockets of a skeleton. He stopped breathing, and felt himself trembling uncontrollably. And that made him all the more desperate to empty his bladder. There was nothing to be done about that, but a moment's thought reassured him about the skeleton. Of course! Arbuthnot was a doctor.

Defoe had no fear of old bones, but he did worry about rattling it again, just as he worried about jangling the bottles and jars ranged around his feet. Not knowing how long he might be stuck inside, he sought as comfortable a position as possible and breathed deeply.

To the upright, there ariseth a light in darkness. And so it was for Defoe. The cupboard doors were glazed but also curtained with some kind of muslin. Once his eyes had adjusted, he found that he commanded through that gauzy barrier a view of the nearest parts of Dr Arbuthnot's salon. He heard the door open, and after a moment a man's voice said, 'There is nobody here. Come on, and we'll fetch ourselves a drink.' The speaker moved towards the bureau where he opened a door. He had his back to Defoe, but made the unmistakable sound of a cork being pulled from a flask. 'Here, pass me one of those,' said the man.

A woman replied: 'These aren't for drinking, they're cupping glasses.'

'Well, I think it's an honour to have such a noble vessel, so recently peeled off the Queen's royal arse.'

'I shall give mine a good wipe first, if you don't mind.'

Defoe heard the sound of liquor being poured, then silence as they drank, followed by conspiratorial laughter. 'Here, let's have another.'

Then the woman said, 'You can if you like. There are guards looking everywhere for a murderer. They may come in at any time. Is Mr Pope coming here tonight?'

'Does he scare you?'

'Don't be foolish. He's the sweetest man, gives me a smile when he arrives and a penny when he leaves. How could a man like that scare me?'

'He's not always so gentle when speaking about your sex,' said the man. 'I don't trust him.'

It was wrong, the man argued, for any Catholic to be allowed access to the castle. He might try to assassinate the Queen, like the Frenchie who'd nearly done for Lord Oxford. The woman rejected this argument. 'Mr Pope is too frail for anything so rough. In fact, I rather like him. A man like that must be looking for a good woman to be his wife . . .'

'Do you mean you, you saucy baggage? Why, a man like that would never marry you.'

'Don't speak about things you don't understand,' she replied. 'I have seen the way he looks at me. And I take care to have him catch me looking back, then look away shyly. Just you wait and see . . .'

They were interrupted by the sound of somebody else arriving outside. Defoe watched them hurriedly replace the cupping glasses on the table and shut the door of the bureau, then heard a clattering at the fireplace.

The door opened. 'Thank you,' said the newcomer, in a piping voice like that of a child. 'Thank you, thank you, thank you. That's so very, very kind of you.'

'Here you are, Mr Pope,' said the manservant. 'Let's just move these chairs and you can make yourself comfortable here by the fire.' Defoe heard the sound of furniture being pushed about and watched Pope drop into his chair, the crutches rattling to the floor beside him.

The maid brought over a couple more candles, by which additional light Defoe saw much that he'd missed earlier. A stuffed crocodile hung from the ceiling over the table. Tiny Egyptian mummies, represented on their front by eagles, stood on a shelf opposite, alongside several vast jars containing pickled abortions and freakish infants. The horrid thought crossed Defoe's mind that these might be the Queen's children, but then he checked himself. It didn't matter whose they were, for the only certainty was that they were somebody's. Defoe's wife too had lost babies – whose had not? – and he could well imagine the miserable story behind each preserved child. An excellent subject for a book, perhaps, but a dismal setting for Pope to wait in.

'Now,' the maid said, 'is there anything we can fetch you while you wait for the doctor and the other gentlemen? I can't imagine they will keep you much longer.'

She leaned right over Pope, shoving her bosom before his face as she smoothed the tablecloth in front of him.

Pope asked for a dish of tea. He expressed the polite hope that, if the doctor had been kept busy with the Queen, he would soon aid her to full recovery. The maid said this was a fine sentiment that she was sure they all shared, and with great impertinence she patted the little poet on his knee.

When she'd gone, Pope let out a deep sigh.

He was widely believed to be positioning himself as Poet Laureate under the Pretender. That charge, innocuous enough in itself, was hard either to prove or dismiss. It could not be surprising, would even be forgivable, if privately Pope did wish for the Pretender to take the crown: after all, he endured the same restrictions as other Catholics.

But for Defoe, those restrictions seemed entirely right. The Church of Rome commanded a force of believers disposable at once for service, however disagreeable. The experience of twelve hundred years, the ingenuity of forty generations of statesmen in Rome, had improved Catholic policy to such perfection that, among the contrivances which have been devised for deceiving and oppressing mankind it occupied the highest place. It was entirely likely that Pope, despite appearing mild and inoffensive, formed a part of that brutal engine. But despite looking into the matter, Defoe had been unable to establish that Pope used anything more practical than prayer to advance the cause of the Pretender.

Pope stayed at St James's with the painter Jervas. They spent mornings together in the studio, where Pope watched closely the spoiled young women who sat for portraits. Much of what he saw was said to have gone directly into 'The Rape of the Lock', the poem that had made Pope rich. Even the Queen, not known as a great reader, was said to have enjoyed it. Every writer envied him.

Until recently, Pope spent his evenings at Buttons' coffee house, where the other regulars included Addison, Steele and the amiable

Nick Rowe, but Pope had drifted away from Buttons', and Defoe had not been able to find out where he went, until Pope wrote again in the *Spectator*, proposing the publication of a 'Works of the Unlearned', a parodic counterpart to a contemporary journal entitled, no less absurdly, 'Works of the Learned'. A group of authors would collaborate in drawing up a mock biography of one Martin Scriblerus, a lunatic polymath who dipped into everything and understood nothing. Together, they called them-selves the Scriblerus Club and were said to meet at court. Only now did Defoe conclude that they met here, in the rooms that belonged to Dr Arbuthnot.

On any other night he would have been delighted to infiltrate the group. As a writer, he ached for a share of their renown, but the events of the previous hour gave him reason to suppose he might never write again.

Even at the best of times he would never exactly have wel-comed standing inside a cupboard while a crippled poet dreamed by the fireside. To do so tonight was torture. The skeleton leered beside him, his feet tingled, the veins in his calves ached. He wrig-gled his toes and shifted his weight from one leg to the other. After fifteen minutes, he felt an intense need to make water. And with every minute that passed the likelihood increased that the Queen's guard would be after him – and not with spaniels but a pack of the drooling hounds he'd spotted at the entrance. If he was caught, there would be beatings before he was thrown in jail; Nottingham had plenty of brutes working for him who would be eager to avenge their dead colleague.

But it was not himself Defoe worried for. It was his wife. He pictured Sarah in some rich man's house after he was gone, down on her knees scrubbing the floor while the rich man watched her backside as it waved in the air and trembled with the hard push of her shoulders.

But then something happened to put an end to the agony. Pope had disappeared from view. And now he was calling out for help.

*They all laughed heartily, even little Pope, wishing to
seem a man of the world*

Chapter 12

A Dreary Subject

Pope must have slipped off his chair. He lay almost horizontal. After waiting a moment, he called again, only louder. Soon he was shouting at the top of his voice, and grabbing one of his crutches from the floor he banged that too. 'Help!' he cried. 'Help! Please help me!'

Defoe felt a strong urge to leap out of his cupboard. Had the man seen him? But there was nothing Defoe could do. To explain how he got into the cupboard in the first place would be impossible.

The light emitted by the fire was still dim, hardly more than the glow of embers. Not knowing what was going on, Defoe could only silently join Pope in praying that somebody would soon hear his calls for help. He might then find an opportunity to escape from this idiotic confinement.

Mercifully, the manservant arrived at once with Pope's tea. From the door he saw the little body wriggling by the fireside and put down the dish to help. Shortly after, several other voices were heard in the corridor. One evidently belonged to Arbuthnot, who took over from the servant in helping his friend up. Defoe also heard the name Gay, and the Irish accent of another man. He peered eagerly through the cracks for a sighting of the Pretender, but none of the men who arrived possessed those haunting features. So he took advantage of the commotion by loosening his breeches, carefully raising a jar from the floor and blending with the herbal remedies inside it, as quickly as he could manage, a powerful stream of hot urine.

And then he was really shocked. The newcomers brought with them enough light to filter through the curtains lining the cupboard. Turning aside, Defoe found that, in addition to the skeleton, he kept company with the naked, pickled body of a young man. It had a waxy pallor, no hair at all, not even on the private parts, and glass eyes.

Defoe thought he might be sick, and breathed deeply to prevent it. He turned his body towards the cadaver, as if ready to ward off any sudden movement, and looked out on the room to get a better view of the people who'd come in. The one with an Irish accent he recognised from the ball. The others called him Parnell.

Gay was younger, and chubby-faced. Arbuthnot, who carried his wig under his arm like a toy dog, had darkish hair, though not much of it on top. His nose was short and tilted upwards, so that the first things a person would notice on meeting him were the nostrils. He had small, dark eyes that only added to the pig-like effect.

So here they were, the Scriblerus Club. Defoe knew little about Gay, but it was safe to say that this gathering of Scotsman, Irishman and Catholic could hardly be friendly towards Protestant Englishmen. Whether that amounted to a plot to impose the Pretender remained to be seen, but after so long reproaching himself for coming to these chambers, Defoe allowed himself congratulations.

Settling back in his seat, Pope assumed an expression of great seriousness and asked Arbuthnot about the Queen's health. The doctor said he'd been with her an hour ago. 'Her Majesty has not much longer to live. Women, like linen, look best by night, but even the dimmest candlelight can't conceal the Queen's sickness. I have shaved the hair at the back of her head and let blood for fifteen minutes.'

'My dear doctor,' said Gay, 'you have expressed the same gloomy view of the Queen's health for many months, if not longer. In a manner of speaking, you are right: we're all dying in the long run. But consider the errors you have made in the past and remember that your current prognosis may be no less mistaken. The Queen may yet survive for years.'

'I have, it's true, made mistakes before now,' Arbuthnot conceded, 'but this time I am certain. At best, Her Majesty has only a few weeks. Every day her condition worsens. I often wonder, on waking at night, if she hasn't died in her sleep.'

'This is a dreary subject,' said Parnell. 'Can we speak of something else?'

He took from a parcel of papers a sheet of vellum that he held up before his audience as though it were the weapon in a murder case. Looking sternly at Pope, he started to read from the sheet in Latin. It took a few moments for them all to recognise it. When Parnell had finished, he turned to Pope again.

'Mr Pope, to the charge of plagiarism, how do you plead?' He took a sip from his glass. He drank slowly, like a connoisseur, lingering on the taste.

Pope recognised the passage – how could he not? – but he was lost for words. Parnell put down his drink and stood up. 'I have smoked out Mr Pope's thievery,' he said, his face flushed with triumph. 'The vellum came from an ancient order of monks in

Ireland. Mr Pope somehow got hold of it, translated it and shoved it into his 'Rape of the Lock' as if it were his own. Is that not shocking?'

Pope smiled weakly. He had done no such thing, but couldn't account for Parnell's manuscripts. Saliva flooded into his mouth as he considered the best response. At last he was obliged to swallow, producing a shift in his Adam's apple that Parnell correctly interpreted as a token of discomfort.

'Hah! Got you!' Parnell rose from his seat again, applauding himself before patting the little poet on the shoulder. 'An excellent joke, was it not?'

Pope still smiled, but said nothing till Parnell finished explaining: he had committed to memory a passage of verse that Pope had recited weeks before, then gone away to translate it into Latin. Having done that, he'd paid a man to write it out on vellum, and the joke was complete.

Arbuthnot made an effort to restore Pope's mood. 'You have not eaten,' he said. 'I'm ashamed. Will you have some pie?'

Pope said he would, so Arbuthnot ordered a footman to bring a huge pigeon pie. Then they set about drinking great quantities of liquor, Parnell especially.

The pie arrived, carried by an ancient servant who looked as if he must have served many generations of Stuarts.

'Gentlemen, handle your arms,' Arbuthnot said, gesturing towards the knives and forks.

'Don't cut like a mother-in-law,' said Parnell. 'Send me a huge slice. And tell me, does anybody know the age of the fellow who brought it here? He looked as old as Methuselah.'

Nobody replied.

Defoe had eaten hardly anything. Watching them eat was fresh torture.

After a moment, Parnell looked up. 'He was an ingenious man that first found out eating and drinking,' he said.

'You have not eaten much,' said Arbuthnot.

'Doctor, do you not see all the bones on my plate? They say a carpenter is known by his chips.' After a pause, he waved his knife in the air. 'I could dispose of your pie much faster if it were not for this. It's so blunt, I could ride to London on it without suffering the least discomfort.'

'Well perhaps you had better,' said Gay. 'There is no horse dealer will come after you for the price of that old thing.'

'You have heard of my little problem, then?' Parnell took a pistol from his coat pocket and placed it on the table before him. 'And what have you done to look after your own debts, my wise friend?'

Gay said nothing but looked a little ashamed. Arbuthnot answered for him. 'Mr Gay has secured himself employment. Have you not heard? He's to be Envoy Extraordinary to the new Ambassador to Hanover.'

Gay looked down, fiddled with the buttons on his coat.

'Is that right?' asked Parnell, whose jocular style seemed less natural now. 'The least ambitious of our group, and the one best able to accept whatever fate deals him. So perhaps we shall all need to learn German after all.'

'What about you, Pope? What will you do to secure yourself?' asked Parnell.

'I shall be busy for a long while, translating the *Iliad*.'

'But only if you raise enough money first,' said Parnell. 'You have had your two guineas from me, but I've no more to give you. I wish you luck, but people are too busy preparing for the Queen's death to think about the fall of Troy.'

'We can never be too busy to study the past,' said Arbuthnot. 'How else can we hope to understand the present, or plan for the future?'

'I make no attempt to understand, or prepare for anything,' said Parnell. 'You are better men than me.'

'Are you raising the money you need?' Gay asked.

'Not enough,' Pope replied. 'Not yet. I can never do it on my own. I rely on my friends – not just for your money, though that is most welcome, Parnell, but for urging others to subscribe too. Swift has been tireless in my cause.'

'And Jervas, I hear,' said Arbuthnot. 'He never paints a young lady's portrait without urging her parents to fund your Homer.'

'He has been very kind.'

'But Mr Addison has done little for you,' said Parnell.

'He gave me the courage to start my work . . .'

'But after that – nothing! The Whigs have abandoned you, Pope, and I fear that you can never raise the money without them.'

'You may be right. But I hope my friends will see me through. In the meantime, I am editing Shakespeare's plays.'

'It has been done.'

'But not well. I shall remove passages that demean the Bard. How could such a genius put into the mouth of Hector an allu‑ sion to Aristotle, who lived hundreds of years after the war of Troy?'

'I am agog.'

'He did not,' Pope said. 'The text has been corrupted.'

'Forget Shakespeare,' said Parnell. 'He's overrated. His historical plays are merely redressing of older plays on the same subjects and the finest things are taken verbatim. You might think that, "A horse, a horse, my kingdom for a horse" was Shakespeare's. Not a syllable!'

'Our own Queen's story would have appealed to Shakespeare, if he'd lived to see it,' said Gay.

'That old man who brought us our supper might have met Shakespeare,' said Pope. But Parnell didn't seem to hear him. He was thinking of what Gay said.

'An ungrateful daughter,' Parnell whispered, flirting with treason.

'And the watery banishment of the King and his little child?' said Arbuthnot, lowering his head as if he expected a blow from an invisible schoolmaster behind him. Defoe could hardly contain his joy to hear such treachery.

Pope made no comment, but took a booklet from his coat and, having reached behind him for Arbuthnot's quill, made a note in it. For a while nobody spoke. Then Pope suggested that, now they had all eaten, it might be time to address the main purpose of their meeting.

At last! Now perhaps Defoe would find out the information he needed.

But Arbuthnot said it would be better to wait till everybody involved in their scheme had arrived. 'Or does anybody have any other ideas?'

Did this mean the Pretender might finally appear?

'I'll tell you a funny thing,' said Gay, eager to put behind him the awkwardness about his appointment.

'Allow us to be the judges of that,' Parnell quickly replied.

'I had a conversation the day before yesterday with a Drury Lane whore . . .'

Parnell whistled suggestively, but Gay continued.

'I wanted to know about her trade, and how it was that she kept busier than the rest. "Sir," she said, "the secret is easy to relate. You must not forget to use the natural accent of dying persons, and add to the sighs and pleasure." Though in truth, she told me, "if you follow the trade long enough, you'll be no more moved by an embrace than if you were made of stone or wood." Well, I could have guessed as much, but I scolded the minx all the same for she had used the same accents and sighs and pleasantries not ten minutes earlier on me!'

'What did she say to that?' asked Parnell.

'She said it was always a great pleasure to serve a gentleman. Now, this struck me as the most obvious lie, so I asked what she meant. If I am a gentleman, what could her other customers be like? But this time I could not have guessed at her answer. She said, "It is odds-on, sir, that most men, when they get in bed, will climb aside my back and demonstrate how they managed their horse at Blenheim." Well I ask you, friends, does this sound famil-iar? Am I the only man among us who does not do that?'

They all laughed heartily, even little Pope, wishing to seem a man of the world like the rest. The merriment was interrupted by the arrival of Oxford, who begged the gentlemen not to get up. He was accompanied by Jonathan Swift, and a man Defoe didn't recognise. The Lord Treasurer walked around the table, taking care to shake each man's hand and look him firmly in the eye as he declared himself delighted to see him.

Defoe, still hiding, was appalled. Moments before, he had been congratulating himself on infiltrating a circle of Catholics, High Anglicans and supporters of the Pretender. Now it seemed he was among the friends of his patron. He had made a terrible mistake.

Arbuthnot couldn't think of a good way to tell the Queen
she was not going to live much longer

Chapter 13

The Queen's Dead Children

Lady Masham returned as fast as she could to her rooms, with Mary hurrying behind her. Lady Masham looked disturbed by the news of the Queen's unprecedented visit. What had the queen discovered in her rooms? Was she going to be dismissed, removed from her powerful position like the Duchess of Marlborough before her?

The Duchess, refusing to accept her removal, had come banging on the Queen's door to demand an explanation, and the Queen had been obliged to shout back, 'You can put it in writing,' – a line that for some time afterwards, in certain circles, had only to be uttered once to induce hysterical laughter.

They passed through a series of corridors, each one thronged with servants rushing to deal with the demands of the Queen's guests. When they saw Lady Masham coming, the servants stopped moving and stood with their backs to the wall. They might not do that much longer, Mary thought, if the Queen has found out about Lady Masham's thefts. But there had been nothing to suggest that about the Queen's manner when Mary accompanied her to Lady Masham's rooms.

As they walked, Mary heard music and sudden laughter and conversation echoing up the stairwells. Would she ever rejoin the ball? If not, when would she see Samuel again? It was not easy for him to get away from home, and there were few opportunities as good as this to meet without attracting attention.

She was still dreaming when they reached Lady Masham's rooms.

'What's the matter?'

Mary didn't want to say. Somebody as cold-hearted as Lady Masham couldn't possibly understand. 'I'm sorry. It's nothing.'

'Is it love?' There was something scornful about Lady Masham's use of the word. 'You don't believe your father will let you see Samuel Holland?'

Mary was astonished that Lady Masham knew who he was. But she would not allow her to triumph in the knowledge. She just shrugged, as if to say the reason for her father's dislike was obvious. 'Well, he's a Whig.'

Lady Masham tapped her on the arm with her fan. 'Marry somebody else. If you want him enough, Holland will still be yours.' Then they stepped inside.

The Queen was lying on her bed, her chest rising and falling as she breathed heavily. A single candle burned on the dressing table beside her. Mary went to the far end of the room and stood by quietly. Lady Masham walked towards the bulky figure, wrapped in a heavy cloak and bandaged around the head where Arbuthnot had breathed a vein before they came here. Her eyes were closed. Having assured herself that the Queen was sleeping, Lady Masham walked around the room in a frenzy looking behind drapes and under tables. Then she kneeled down to look under the covers of her bed. She had obviously found what she was looking for, because she sighed with relief – and then she started singing, on her knees.

Was it the stolen money?

Several minutes passed. Mary wondered if Lady Masham had forgotten she was even there. But then Lady Masham turned to her and whispered something so shocking that Mary thought she must have misheard. 'How easy it would be,' she said, 'to put the Queen out of her misery. Why let her suffer any longer? We could smother her now, perhaps without even waking her.'

What could Mary say? Had the Queen heard? Lady Masham needed the Queen alive; surely no successor would look on her so kindly? But perhaps Lady Masham believed her thefts had been discovered, and felt it was better to lose her patron than her reputation.

It may only have been Mary's horrified expression that made Lady Masham laugh. 'I am jesting, silly girl! Anyway, we need to help her regulate her affairs while she still can. The Queen is struggling to make a difficult decision, and we must help her.'

From outside, in the park, a great cheer rang out. Lady Masham went to the window and pulled aside the curtain. Mary walked across too. In the moonlight they saw a group of beaux racing on piggyback. Despite the many differences between the two ladies in waiting, Mary couldn't help but think how closely their positions resembled that of the riders: powerless themselves and entirely dependent on the progress of somebody else. Lady Masham continued watching for a moment, smiling almost in spite of herself when one man collapsed backwards upon his rider.

It was a pretty smile, because for once it was not forced.

Then Lady Masham crossed the room to the Queen's side. She put a hand on the Queen's arm, stroking it gently till she opened her eyes.

'Your Majesty. It's an honour to see you here. Would Dr Arbuthnot approve?'

The Queen didn't answer immediately but slowly familiarised
herself with the room. She smiled faintly. 'He would disapprove.
But I wanted so much to see your little baby.'

In Cabinet, the day before, the Queen had received a formal
request from the Hanoverian Ambassador, Baron Schutz. This
asked permission for the Elector to send his son to visit Britain and
take his seat in the Lords. The prospect of meeting his son stirred
up strong feelings for the Queen. 'I could not bear to have any
successor here,' the Queen told her chief ministers, 'even if it were
only for a week.' Mary had never seen her so moved. Bolingbroke
had argued against the young man's visit and insinuated that
Oxford had contrived the idea. Oxford denied it, and promised to
speak to Baron Schutz about withdrawing the request.

Still today the Queen seemed to be unhappy. She was taking it
confoundedly hard, Lady Masham said earlier, and must not be
allowed, for her own good, to get beside herself.

But now Lady Masham seemed to have changed her mind,
perhaps she had decided that it might, after all, be useful to
remind the Queen of the relations she had lost? Mary could find
no other explanation for the conversation that followed.

It started with Lady Masham asking Mary to fetch the nurse
and her baby. Mary went to the door and passed the message to a
footman. And when she returned, closing the door quietly behind
her, she heard the Queen speaking about her as if she were no
longer there. Lady Masham gave her a sharp glance that seemed to
say, 'Stay where you are!'

The Queen was asking if Lady Masham had heard Mary's
news. 'I have tried to dissuade her,' the Queen said in a whisper,

'but without success. I told her that her father might have chosen her a wonderful husband. My own dear George was chosen for me and I loved him dearly. He was kind, and handsome, and never kept a mistress. But she says she must marry for love – and she takes you for her example.'

Lady Masham smiled, but said nothing. She moved to the harpsichord and started to play something soothing – a tune of Purcell's that Her Majesty still associated with her late husband. The effect was immediate.

'I dreamed about him again last night,' the Queen said, heaving herself upwards. 'And he seemed so real that when I woke it was as if he had died again.'

Lady Masham stopped playing and turned to listen. 'That must have been terribly dismaying, Your Majesty.'

'It was. I dreamed of our wedding night. I was only a girl, and George was nearly twice my age, but I was pretty enough, then, and he seemed overwhelmed by the achievement of marrying at all. He burst into tears as soon as the court withdrew from our bedchamber. He spent an hour with me, then left to wander round the gardens all night.' She smiled at the memory. Mary often wondered how that first night together would feel. She didn't think Samuel would be shy. Surely, it would be Mary herself who hid under the covers and blushed.

'After that dream, I woke and felt a fresh sense of bereavement,' the Queen said.

Lady Masham could perhaps understand the strong feelings, but Mary doubted that she had ever felt anything like them herself. She once heard her say that the chief benefit of her own husband, now that she had secured her position, was that she could count the hours pass at night by his snores.

'I dreamed of the little ones, too.' Then the Queen began to reel off a list of her losses, the paralysing atrocity of motherhood. 'I dreamed they had all come back, each babe alive again — the ones that died before they were born, the ones that died soon after, and the beautiful, beautiful darlings who survived a while longer.' She spoke slowly. Mary was reminded how much she had always admired the Queen, not pitied her as others supposed. 'They would all be adult now, if they had lived, and that's how they were in my dream, with faces that I'd never seen before, but oddly familiar. I suppose they resembled me, or my sister, God love her, or dear George. Perhaps there was even something of my father, may the Lord have mercy upon his soul.'

'Did you dream of your father too?'

'No, no I did not. Not exactly. But I — I have always believed they died because of him.'

Lady Masham raised her eyebrows in surprise.

'This must be terribly boring for you.'

'Not at all, Your Majesty. I only wish that by talking about them we could bring them back. Please, tell me about them again.' Mary wondered what Lady Masham was trying to do — bring the Queen to a fresh sense of distress?

'Will you have some brandy?' asked Lady Masham, rising.

'Not now. I had somebody bring me a bottle,' she said, gesturing towards a nearby table. 'And as you see I have drunk a little already. But I take too much of it.'

Lady Masham sat down again.

'My first was a girl, born at St James's Palace. She lived for just one day but I was so proud of her, and George was too. She had thick black hair that stood up like a brush. It broke our hearts to bury her. The second, named Princess Mary after my sister, lived for twenty months. She died of smallpox just days after the baby girl who was born after her, Anne Sophia.'

'What was she like, little Mary?' Lady Masham had heard it all before, but Bolingbroke had reminded her what benefits accrued from listening sympathetically.

'Oh, she was always laughing. And full of mischief. But after one of the servants told her that her sister had died, she never smiled again.'

Lady Masham stroked the Queen's hand again. 'And court tradition deprived you of any keepsake . . .'

'That's right.'

'Heartbreaking . . . Could you recover nothing from the girls' governess?'

'I couldn't ask. And the governess never thought to offer anything.' The Queen looked shattered, but Lady Masham seemed to want her to continue, so she did.

'Later that same year, I had a son, after long labour, who died in the process. His arm appeared first, and swelled monstrously so that a surgeon had to cut it off before inducing the rest, the next day, by feeding me portions of spoiled rye.'

'You poor woman. I thank God I never endured such brutality.'

'They thought I would die too, after that. The shock alone would kill most women, not to mention the bleeding. I thought it would never stop. But somehow I survived, just as I miraculously survived the raging bout of smallpox that killed so many at court when I was a girl. The Lord preserved me – though only He knows why.

'Next came little William, named Duke of Gloucester, who was always sickly, and more babies who died on the day they were born, with scarcely enough time to be baptised, poor souls. A boy, a girl, another girl, a boy, another boy, and finally a girl.'

'The last two, you told me, were delivered by Peter Chamber-len, using his secret forceps machine. He brought it to the confinement in a carved, gilded box . . .'

The Queen nodded, but Lady Masham had judged badly. The Queen was not in the mood to elaborate on such technicality. But after a few moments, she spoke again.

'Looking back,' she said, 'you might think I would have pre-pared myself for each loss after so many had died before. But I didn't. When you carry a baby you always believe it will survive. You think, this time it will be different. And each time the pres-sure is greater than the last and the loss more bitter.

'Children are a heritage of the Lord, and the fruit of the womb is His reward . . . I will multiply thy seed as the stars in heaven, the Lord says, and as the sand which is on the sea shore. But after seventeen pregnancies, all we had left was the little Duke of Gloucester. He used to sit with me and hold my hand, he was always holding my hand, and tell me his plans for the baby broth-ers and sisters he felt sure would come soon. I couldn't tell him that I was too old to produce any more.'

Mary found that she was clenching her fists, as if by doing so she could help the Queen to withstand Lady Masham's onslaught of sympathy. She felt in her pocket for the rosary her father had given her, and clenched those tight too.

'Then William fell into a fever on his eleventh birthday after too much dancing. We stood beside him on his bed and waited with him as he passed in and out of wakefulness. He said dancing was important, kept saying it, and wanted the doctor to come back like he'd done so many times previously and make things better, but we could only smile because the doctor told us there was nothing more he could do. And William asked why did people smile at him so? He always liked his father best, he told me himself, but he loved my hands, he said, and I held his hand in mine while he slipped away. He felt damp, and talked about grass, but I don't know what he meant by it. He said it was time to go into the next room, where there was more light, and he could hear people's voices, but there was nobody.

'Now I have nobody. Nobody but you, dearest Abigail.' Lady Masham shot a glance towards Mary, perhaps supposing she would feel hurt. She didn't. But the Queen's remark showed how gravely she was in the power of Lady Masham, and how much she needed Mary. It also showed how little Mary's word would count for if she ever opposed the older lady-in-waiting.

'It's the quiet times I miss them most,' the Queen continued. 'When I'm lonely and they might have kept me company. To think that I'll never sit with them again and hear them play and laugh . . . it's too painful even to say it.'

She stared at the ceiling for several moments, close to tears. 'My poor babies. My little princes and princesses — I know their blessed souls can hear me, can hear their miserable mother. They are with us now, Abigail. They are with their mother who loves them. Every day I pray to them to intercede for me. To beg God for a grave to hide my bones, so I don't have to rest them any longer on this awful bed.'

An expression of mild surprise flashed involuntarily across Lady Masham's face. The Queen happened to see it, remembered whose bed she lay on, and smiled weakly. 'Of course, dear Abigail, it's my own bed that is awful. Yours has been a happy place, productive of the most wonderful children . . .'

With immense effort, the Queen started to climb slowly off the bed in question. 'We're taught to show forbearance,' she said, staggering heavily, like a child taking its first steps. Lady Masham supported her, noticing as she did so that the Queen's bandaged head had leaked blood copiously on to her clean sheets of white Holland. 'We're taught that no misfortune is so horrible that we will not be strong enough to cope if it happens to us. That we'll grapple with our misfortune and find ourselves stronger than we ever supposed ourselves to be. But that's not been my experience. I pray constantly – so why am I unable to deal with my loss?'

The Queen lowered herself to the floor in a kneeling position, hands pressed together before her on the bed. Lady Masham swiftly moved beside her, then sat on the bed, to the Queen's astonishment. Mary remembered the thing under the bed. Lady Masham was trying to hide it! But the Queen continued her prayer.

'May Almighty God have mercy on William's soul,' she began, breathless again and barely audible. 'And on Mary's soul. And on the souls of little George and Anne Sophia. And on the other tiny ones who fell asleep no sooner than they opened their eyes. And may He have mercy on my soul, who brought their deaths on them.'

For a long time, nobody spoke.

'I blame myself,' the Queen said. 'I betrayed my father and my little half-brother.'

For a brief instance, Lady Masham looked astonished. The Queen had never spoken about the Pretender like this.

'The boy was to be a Catholic, like our father, and he would take precedence over his Protestant sisters. I took care to absent myself from the birth, and when people started to gossip that he was not legitimate – was smuggled into the chamber in a warming pan merely to impose a Catholic succession on an unwilling nation – I kept silent. And when my father fled the country, fearing the worst of the antiCatholic mob, I did nothing. I have never told anybody this before, but dear Abigail . . .'

Lady Masham nodded.

'From his exile in France, my father wrote me a letter containing his bitterest curse, and from that time onward I started to lose my children. Not one of them survived. Only a fool would believe this coincidence.'

She put her hands over her face and her body started to shake. She buried her face in the bedclothes and sobbed loudly.

Lady Masham observed the Queen's shudders and calculated that she had time to step towards the sideboard and help herself to a slice of the cheese. This she did, rousing the attention of two lapdogs, a spaniel and a Pekingese, that had seemed asleep. They stood and shook themselves with an air of expectation. The Queen continued to mutter and shake slightly, but paid no attention to the movement of the little dogs. After Lady Masham had consumed a few mouthfuls, her baby daughter arrived. The nurse, first curtseying to the prone figure of her sovereign, handed the precious bundle to its mother. And Lady Masham, having helped the Queen into a chair, passed her tiny infant to the Queen. She was awake, mewling and jerking her arms and legs uncontrollably as she was removed from her swaddling.

'She has beautiful eyes,' the Queen said. 'Like your dear husband's.'

But this was Bolingbroke's.

She went on to express her admiration at the baby's wrinkled hands and feet, with their papery, overgrown nails. She admired the soft, smooth skin, the milky smell, the tightly closed eyes as the baby cried, and the wide-open mouth that puckered and turned hungrily to one side. 'This baby needs feeding,' she told Lady Masham, who feigned uncertainty on this obvious fact to flatter her royal visitor. 'She wants the Queen of England to feed her! Forgive me but I can't provide what you need, beautiful child.' The wet-nurse stepped forward.

Afterwards, the Queen took her back and held her upright to let out the wind.

Lady Masham watched nervously. She had never believed – as others did – that the Queen's bad luck was infectious, capable of killing any child she so much as laid hands on. But who could say for sure that she would not one day, out of rage and jealousy, fling a healthy baby from her, smashing its brains out?

'Nursing a baby is troublesome,' the Queen said to the nurse. 'It ruins your clothes, makes you look old, and can be a danger to your health. But it affords many convenient moments of peace for prayer. I hope you pray often when you feed this child.' The nurse indicated that she did little else. 'Then you shall have your reward in heaven, if not on earth. My own nurse, Martha Farthing, fed me for fifteen months, and I never forgot her. On my accession, I gave her a pension of three hundred pounds. You should remember that.' The nurse promised to do so. 'And take care not to fall asleep and crush her while she feeds.'

After a few moments, the Queen started to weep again. She was thinking of her oldest boy. 'Poor William! He never was a strong child.' Lady Masham had never seen the little Duke, but from what she heard, he was an ugly boy, pasty-faced and swollen-headed.

'The day before he died, he called to me and said no matter

how much I loved him I must pass on the crown to somebody else. I must not hate them for not being him. Next day the sun rose as usual, as if nothing terrible had happened. I remember it exactly, because we sat at his bedside for hours, beside his pale body, watching the dawn. George had not wanted to believe he was dead, but a mother knows, George was not certain, he always refused to face how badly things looked, always searched for a cheerful word. But a mother knows. Everything was black, black, black, and from that time onwards I had no more caresses from my children nor from George either. I didn't want him in my bed. All I could think was that I should have taken lovers, with stronger seed, and I could not bear the sight of him. And my prayers were hollow, and I muttered them without believing a word I said, until the Lord taught me to love him better by taking George from me too. How much I missed him then!'

She paused. 'The Lord has kept me alive for a reason, but I still don't know what it is.'

'Madam,' said Lady Masham, taking back her daughter and letting out a sigh that might, just conceivably, be interpreted by the Queen as pitying. 'I know a mother whose child was not half so good as yours – not beautiful, not good, not clever, he brought pain to her heart all his life. But no mother ever wept more than she did for this boy after he died.'

This observation failed to produce great relief. The Queen buried her head in her hands.

So Lady Masham changed tack. 'Another woman, who buried four little ones in a year, told me she has more pleasure thinking of those four than of any living child who grew up to have families of their own and forget her.'

The Queen sat up, her face flushing redder than before, to point out that none of her own children had lived to disappoint her.

Lady Masham's patience was failing her. She had been listening attentively for a long time, and having achieved the tearful outburst she intended, now seemed to find the Queen merely exasperating.

'Well, Madam. We must learn to accept God's will, no matter how dreadful it seems at the time. You must pull yourself together, Your Majesty. Death strikes us all, and we must not let ourselves take it too badly if others die before us. If somebody is tired and goes to lie down, we do not pursue him with shouting and bawling. Those you have lost have only gone to lie down for a while. You must remember your friends that are alive . . . and those relations you still have.'

The Queen looked at her, unsure how to interpret that pointed advice. After holding the baby again, then handing her back – then asking to hold her once more – the Queen recovered her customary mood of resignation.

She asked Lady Masham to fetch a Bible and to read aloud a passage in Revelation. As she did so, the Queen interrupted, reciting the passage by heart. 'They shall hunger no more,' she said, 'Neither thirst any more. Neither shall the sun light on them. And God shall wipe away all tears from their eyes.'

'He used to sit with me and hold my hand,' the Queen said.
'He was always holding my hand.'

Chapter 14

Priceless Impertinence

'My lord,' said Arbuthnot, welcoming the Lord Treasurer to his rooms. 'It's an honour to see you again. We had started to believe you would never come. How did you find Her Majesty?'

But Oxford had not, as they assumed, been with the Queen. He'd bumped into Swift on the stairs, and then been joined, unwillingly, by a shabby fellow who called himself General Robert Hunter.

'Hunter? I thought you were in America?' said Gay.

Hunter looked delighted to be recognised.

'I returned from New York, at some hazard, as soon as I heard that England is in upheaval.' He added that he wanted to improve his acquaintance with the men who would matter in future – not to renew it with those who were on their way out.

'The last time we met, sir, you told me your scheme to settle the American colonies with a lot of Germans. You set off, as I recall, with some three thousand. Was the journey a success?'

'A great success. We lost a few elderly passengers, but gained plenty of newborns.'

'These Germans had lost their homes to the French, is that right?'

'You have astounding powers of memory.'

'And you put them to work?'

The general nodded.

'Wonderful, wonderful,' said Gay. 'As you know, we shall be settling a few Germans here, soon. Perhaps you can advise how we can bring that off with best success.'

General Hunter sighed. 'Germans are good Christians, sir, and hard workers, but they are not easy to control. Soon after we arrived a portion of them abandoned me to establish their own settlement many miles inland, at a place the Mohawk people call Schoharie.'

'Could you not fetch them back?'

'That's harder to achieve in America, sir, than you ... than many would imagine who have never been there. Schoharie County lies a great distance inland. No roads lead there, only Indian footpaths. When they arrived, they had little to eat but boiled grass and leaves off the trees ... but last year they produced their own crop of wheat. They had to carry it twenty miles to grind it, at Schenectady, but their celebrations surpassed any others I have heard of.'

Gay looked around him and saw that his friends' smiles looked forced. They didn't share his interest in the American.

But the General, not noticing, persisted in his onslaught. 'The Queen, in her wisdom, supposing these Germans to be handsomely settled sent her agent to grant deeds of land. This agent arrived at last and issued an order that householders come to him with details of the land they owned. The poor ignorant souls were struck like with thunder! Alarmed by the appearance of the Queen's agent – he had lost an eye some years previously – they supposed his command was a trick to get themselves under the hateful yoke of tyrannical landholders, to be again enslaved, so soon after they'd tasted liberty. In short, they resolved to kill him.

'The next morning, they surrounded his house, carrying guns, pitch-forks and hoes, demanding him alive or dead. On refusal, they fired sixty balls through the roof. He, having brought pistols, fired back. But when night came on, the Germans dispersed and the agent left the house in the dark to begin the long journey to Schenectady. From there . . .'

'There is more?' asked Swift, only barely stifling a yawn.

Over several minutes, Defoe watched Swift closely. Swift's eyes scanned Hunter from head to foot just a little too slowly for good manners, then he went through an entire repertoire of hostility: checking his pocket watch, pointedly stuffing his mouth with breath-freshening pastillos, even holding a mouchoire over his nose without draining it.

Oblivious, Hunter continued. 'Oh yes, the story is wonderful. From Schenectady, he sent a sheriff to apprehend the ringleaders, but the German women fell upon him, knocked him down, broke his ribs, pissed in his face and deprived him of his other eye – so that when he finally returned to Mr Bayard they presented a spec-tacle that, as you can imagine, was at once horrid and ridiculous.'

'Extraordinary,' said Swift, withholding his smile entirely, as talented a killer of anecdote as any man in London.

'Indeed, sir, I thought so too. In fact, I have written a play upon that subject – the first play to be printed in America.' He turned directly to Oxford. 'I brought with me a copy and would be hon-oured beyond all reasonable expectation if you allowed me to dedicate it to you.'

Oxford avoided a direct refusal. 'A general and a playwright too?'

'We who live among savages must be all things at once.'

'I look forward to seeing the play on Drury Lane,' said Oxford. 'Now you must excuse me. It's been a great pleasure hearing your fascinating stories. But I have some business to attend to with my friends. Can you find your own way back to the ball?'

Hunter looked appalled, but smiled and bowed. He turned toward the others, at the table, who beamed back at him. But only Gay bothered to rise from his seat and return the courtesy.

As soon as the door closed, the friends fell about laughing. When it subsided, Swift wondered aloud if they might have pressed the American for two guineas to support Pope's Homer. Then no one wasted a single word more on the man. Instead, Parnell told Oxford about Swift's adventure the previous day, swimming in the Thames with a certain woman friend. 'I believe it was a common whore,' Parnell said, 'but Swift will not admit it. Come, who was it? I know your type . . . was it Welsh Nan Peg the Seaman's Wife? Long-haired Mrs Spencer? She'll do you a bout for a good price, and I know how little you can afford. The Queen of Morocco?'

Swift decided it would be prudent to put an end to the conjecture. 'All right, it was a common whore,' he said. 'But her identity is neither here nor there . . .'

'So anyway,' said Parnell, cutting in, 'Dr Swift walks slowly into the water and just as he gets out of his depth he feels his breeches come loose, and before he can do anything about them they have gone adrift! He spent the best part of an hour swimming underwater before he finally retrieved them.'

Hearing this, Defoe guessed at once that Swift's lover must be Hester Vanhomrigh, the charming woman who'd come to court dressed as a man. She had come to court to urge Swift's cause on Oxford! Swift didn't deserve her. Did Oxford know who she was? Had she spoken to him? Oxford smiled at Parnell, then corrected him. 'You are mistaken. If Dr Swift had gone with a common whore he'd not have been so bashful. I believe there is true love in the case.'

'A little grain of romance,' said Swift, 'is no ill ingredient to preserve and exalt the dignity of human nature.'

Defoe pitied Oxford. How he wasted his time, smiling at these smug jokers! What had any of them done to help him? Swift had written some pamphlets. Defoe had laughed like any man at Swift's best work, even encouraged others to study the pamphlet that discredited Marlborough. But mocking laughter only went so far. Was there anything Swift really believed in?

As if in answer to that question, Swift said, 'The Queen is dying, or so Arbuthnot insists. Even friends of the Pretender must now court the Whigs and their German champion, before it is too late. You have heard, I suppose, that our friend Gay has thrown himself at the Germans. You move to Hanover soon, I believe . . . ?'

Gay nodded, and reached for his glass.

With a sly glance at Oxford, Swift added, 'Unless you write to the Elector yourself, my Lord, it may soon be too late to establish the same close rapport with our future sovereign as you presently enjoy with Her Majesty.'

He looked towards a side table on which stood a chamber pot emblazoned with the royal coat of arms. Lifting the cloth that covered it, Swift peeked inside and drew back with an expression of exaggerated revulsion. He shot a look at Arbuthnot. 'The Queen's . . . ?'

Oxford ignored this pantomime. 'You seem confident that the

135

Elector's succession is assured,' he said. 'But I believe the Pretender has other plans.' He rubbed his nose. 'Anyway, what you propose is impossible. I could not write to the Elector without the Queen's permission, and she hates to speak of her German relatives. Just to mention him is to make her suffer. As Arbuthnot has made clear, she is in no condition for such a conversation.'

This was why Defoe admired Oxford. The man placed no importance on his own position but put the Queen's interests before everything.

'Then you must ask her very gently,' Swift said. He proposed a game. 'Why not practise, tonight, the request you must make to the Queen tomorrow morning?' Swift would pretend to be the Queen, while Oxford need only be himself.

The suggestion met with approval from all round the table. Oxford agreed, too, and moved towards his seat.

'My lord!' said Swift from the chair he'd already taken at the end of the room. He spoke in the high voice of a woman. He held on his head, in lieu of a crown, one of Arbuthnot's cupping glasses. 'It would be best if you continued to stand while address-ing your sovereign.'

His impertinence was remarkable. Even Defoe smiled, despite himself. 'Oh, this is excellent sport, by God!' said Gay.

Oxford took the reproach in good humour, wiping the smile from his face before starting to speak. 'Your Majesty, I have come to ask your gracious permission . . .'

Swift held up a hand. What was he going to say now?

'There is a virtuous man I have often noted in your company,' he said, 'with a cheerful look, a pleasing eye and a most notable carriage. If the Earl of Bolingbroke should be lewdly inclined, he deceives me, for I see virtue in his looks . . . for two years I have endeavoured to reconcile you and the Secretary of State from the quarrel between you, from which all our misfortunes proceed. You once lived under the strongest bonds of friendship, you were in addition supported by a vast majority of the landed interest and the inferior clergy almost to a man, but you have brought the present administration almost to the brink of ruin, together with the cause of church and monarchy committed to your charge.'

Oxford had grinned at the suggestion that Bolingbroke was not 'lewdly inclined' but thereafter his expression became more serious. What Swift said was too close to the truth to be laughed at as a joke. 'When I first saw you together,' Swift carried on, 'I could not fail to notice the great affection you bore each other, so that, notwithstanding the old maxim that court friendships are not of long duration, I was confident that yours would last as long as your lives. But it seems the inventor of that maxim was wiser than I, who lived to see the friendship degenerate into indifference and suspicion, then corrupt into the greatest animosity and hatred.'

Gay chuckled. 'Priceless impertinence, Swift!' He was putting it on. He didn't dare to show how embarrassing this was. Parnell was doing the same — smiling just a little too broadly and hoping that Swift would not continue much longer. Pope sat straight-faced throughout, as if he simply couldn't hear. Defoe remembered watching him at Buttons' coffee house, pulling much the same face when the wits turned their jokes against his faith.

Still speaking in the Queen's voice, Swift changed tack. 'My lord, you have been a great favourer of men of wit and learning. Certainly none of them can be counted among your enemies, if one may judge from the libels and pamphlets printed against you.' At this self-serving joke, there was a great outburst of laughter, as much as anything to release the tension that had built up. 'How do you intend that we should repay your loyal supporters?'

Defoe was shocked by the man's presumption. Swift had made himself a friend of the Lord Treasurer. If he had yet to receive the rewards that usually went with such a position, that can't have been because he had not asked. Defoe felt proud to serve a patron who did not reward friends for their friendship alone.

Swift was still waiting for the Lord Treasurer to answer his question.

Finally Oxford spoke. 'As I have mentioned previously to Your Majesty,' he began, 'there is no respite from the stream of petition-ers for places and pensions, payment of arrears for pensions and salaries and often outright charity.'

It was embarrassing to think that Oxford might really com-plain to the Queen about the beseeching letters he received. Every man in the room had written a letter of that sort – or many letters.

'No pretext for an address of congratulation or condolence is allowed to pass unspoiled,' Oxford continued. 'I don't believe I have ever shown you this.' He paused, and pulled a letter from his pocket. 'I carry it with me everywhere. It begins with condolences on the death, last year, of my daughter, God rest her soul. But see how it changes the subject afterwards. "Sir," it begins. "I condole with your Lordship from the bottom of my heart. But to mention your grief is only to renew it. If you will give me leave, therefore, I will pass from tenderness to generosity and tell you how you may forever oblige one who would be proud to serve you. I hear Mr Webb is either dead or dying. If so, I beg the governance of the Isle of Wight.'

The room erupted with more of the laughter that hides em-barrassment. Only Swift didn't smile. He waited for silence, and observed — still speaking in a woman's voice — that ambition always did oblige men to abandon their dignity, men who climb adopt the same posture as those who creep. Whatever Oxford might say now, Swift added, he had too often allowed his generosity to get the better of him — and in the least deserving cases. 'You appointed Mr Steele to the *Gazette* and freely raised his payment from £50 a year to £300. Now he has turned against you and written impertinently that I must remove you from office. Is that the kind of gratitude you expected?'

Oxford said he had believed Steele to be the best man for the job, at the time, and was indeed disappointed by his ingratitude. 'He seems to have concluded that I shall not be in office for much longer, and wishes to distance himself from me before my removal takes place.'

'He libelled you constantly,' said Swift, 'and only then resigned his office. In that order.'

If Oxford was annoyed by Swift's insolence, he did nothing to show it. At Arbuthnot's suggestion, they swapped roles. Now Swift would play Oxford, and Oxford would be the Queen.

'Depose me!' exclaimed Swift, to subdued laughter as they exchanged places.

In his role as Queen, Oxford immediately launched an attack on the Lord Treasurer, represented by Swift. 'There is a parson you are friends with . . . a man of the cloth but the least devout I have ever heard of. You know him, as I do, to be the author of innumerable lies, vicious and indecent, directed not only at our enemies but at our friends too . . .'

'I wish Your Majesty would take me with you. Who do you mean?'

'The abominable Dr Swift.'

'Your Majesty, I know the man. But to say I know more harm in him than in myself would be to say more than I know.'

'He spends too much time with Bolingbroke, and I believe he is no less depraved. He swims, naked, in the Thames with whores. You must be rid of him.'

Oxford saved the most devastating till last. 'He's not the kind of man I want as a bishop in my church.'

Nobody was laughing now. And that was when the performance ended. A messenger from the Queen arrived to fetch Arbuthnot. The Queen had been visiting Lady Masham, the messenger said, and now she was back in her room she felt weak again.

The party was over.

Arbuthnot departed, conjuring his friends to stay as long as they liked. But Gay and Parnell left with him. Neither Oxford nor Swift said a word. Pope broke the silence by attempting something jovial. But before he had got far, Swift looked at his watch and announced that he must take Pope to the lodgings they shared at Mrs Partridge's. Defoe had passed the place he named. Swift sprang from his chair and put a hand beneath the little poet's arm. Oxford did nothing to make them stay. Rather than protest, Pope submitted meekly to Swift's bustle and departed with him.

Defoe waited till they had gone, then listened for a moment for any other voices. So far as he could tell, only Oxford remained in the room. Should he make himself known? If he did, would Oxford be amused or angry? For some time, Defoe had wished for any opportunity to get out, but since the merriment turned sour he knew Oxford might prefer not to have been overheard. All the same, he could see no greater chance than this of escape without being detected by his enemies. So he pushed at the cupboard door — producing a squeak that attracted the Lord Treasurer's attention.

But just as Defoe leaned his head out, and caught sight of Oxford's face — the eyebrows shooting up in astonishment — another voice could be heard outside, added to those of Pope and Swift. Defoe darted back inside his cupboard as the owner of this new voice pushed open the door, and entered Arbuthnot's room.

Whoever it was, he seemed surprised to find himself alone with Oxford. 'My lord,' said the voice.

'Lord Secretary.' It was Bolingbroke.

'I make no attempt to understand, or prepare for anything,'
said Parnell

Chapter 15

To Make Us be Friends

Bolingbroke was seventeen years younger than Oxford, but they'd once been close friends. At twenty-six, the younger man was appointed Secretary at War in the Godolphin–Marlborough ministry and when Oxford was dismissed from that administration Bolingbroke had resigned in support. He admired the older man – almost worshipped him.

And the respect was mutual. Oxford saw in Bolingbroke a man of immense talent, if a little undisciplined. Returning to power, Oxford had reappointed him to office and given him a lucrative directorship in the new South Sea company. They trusted each other, and before falling out they had taken difficult decisions together.

'Swift told me I should come to Arbuthnot's rooms just now,' said Bolingbroke as he entered. 'I saw him in the passageway and he said the person I needed to see was waiting for me . . . I suppose it's another of his attempts to make us be friends.'

'It looks that way. He left in a hurry when he saw the time.'

'I'm not sure we will be able to satisfy him.' Bolingbroke pulled off his wig, which threw up a small cloud of powder when he dropped it on the table before him. He ran a hand through his cropped hair, kicked off his shoes, sat down in the chair previously occupied by Mr Pope and helped himself to pie.

'No. Nor am I.'

'You, at any rate, could do him a favour,' said Bolingbroke, 'by giving him his mitre. You could do it if you had a mind to. The Queen has only a short time left, and you may soon lose your chance. Swift deserves more from you – from us. You not only fail to advance his promotion, but actively block it. And yet to him you remain a hero.'

'I have done as much as I could,' Oxford replied. 'I feigned ignorance of his hand in a pamphlet that offended most of Scotland's aristocracy. Anyway, the Queen dislikes him.' He paused. 'She will never give Swift the job he wants in England. You, knowing that, do him less service by encouraging those expectations.'

Defoe felt a thrill, familiar to anyone who has heard of a rival's misfortunes. Oxford's words gave him an advantage over Swift. It did him no good to cherish his rivalrous feelings, but he couldn't always help them. He hoped it would not annoy the Lord Treasurer that he had heard this. Surely he knew Defoe was too loyal to embarrass him?

Bolingbroke, draining the dregs of Pope's glass, denied any such awareness of the Queen's feelings towards Swift. 'We, who are reputed to be in your intimacy, have few opportunities of seeing you and none of talking freely with you. Since you are the only channel through which the Queen's pleasure is conveyed, it follows that there is stagnation until you are pleased to open yourself up and set the water flowing.' As he said this, he stared boldly at Oxford rather than looking away as before.

'Well, I'm here now.'

Even at the height of their friendship they had argued. The great difference between them was party politics. Oxford, originally a Whig but now leader of a mostly Tory administration, took the view that no party should be strong enough to dictate policy to the crown. To prevent that, he employed talented men from both parties. 'Party politics is like a whipsaw,' he used to say. 'Whichever extreme may happen to be pulling, the nation is miserably sawn in half.'

Bolingbroke, on the other hand, was a natural Tory who believed government by a single party was most efficient. He urged Oxford to cease dealing with Whigs, and become a Tory himself. But for Oxford this would have been to betray his Nonconformist family.

Several moments passed in silence. Oxford poured more wine, put the bottle away, tilted back his chair, pulled a snuff box from his pocket, changed his mind and put it away again.

Bolingbroke could contain himself no longer. 'You think yourself master of two different interests, both holding you to be theirs and confiding in you as such, and waiting for you to show yourself in their distinct interests; but you have trimmed to both sides for so long that now both sides begin to see themselves ill-treated. As you love neither side, neither side will stand by you. They will be reconciled only to overturn you, and the Whigs who flourished before shall come in again. You must see that the Whigs have declared themselves against us as far as it is possible without going into open revolution. They sided openly with Hanover in regarding with suspicion our peace with France . . .'

To Bolingbroke's mind, you might as well drive a coach with different sized wheels as attempt to govern with both Whig and Tory ministers.

'We came to court in the same disposition as all parties have done: hoping to have the government in our hands, to enjoy great opportunities of rewarding those who helped to raise us here, as well as hurting those who stood in opposition. When we first worked together I supported moderation, thinking that was the best way to advance the interests of our Tory friends. But then the Whigs triumphed at our expense. Now I see that government by party is inevitable, and so long as that is true I would prefer the Tories to the Whigs. Let the game be wrestled out of our hands and I can bear it, but to fool about like children with it till it slips between our fingers to the ground, so that our opponents have only to stoop and pick it up – that would be unbearable.'

Oxford asked what it was, specifically, that Bolingbroke wanted. 'I have better things to do than continue arguing with a man who never sees merit in my views.'

'I most sincerely desire to see your Lordship, as long as I live, at the head of the Queen's affairs and of the Church of England party. To see the administration flourish under your direction, the Queen's reign secured, and effective measures taken to put those of our friends who may outlive the Queen beyond the reach of Whig resentment. These are the only views I have and the only designs I am engaged in.'

Having pulled an assortment of expressions, suggesting astonishment at this implausible declaration of loyalty, Oxford said he believed Bolingbroke was engaged in designs to enrich himself.

Defoe was delighted. Bolingbroke was a rake, disloyal to his wife, and if he could be dishonest in that way then why not in other ways too? Defoe wished dearly to see his patron break with Bolingbroke and form an alliance with the Whigs. If he did, he might even replace Walpole as their leader.

'So far as that goes, I don't deny it,' Bolingbroke said. 'Your Lordship is no different in wishing to secure advantages for yourself and for your family. Before your son's marriage to the daughter of the late Duke of Newcastle, I understand you asked Her Majesty to revive the lapsed title in him . . .'

Defoe cringed, deeply regretting that he should have heard this and wishing he had never stepped inside Dr Arbuthnot's rooms. Was this to be another terrible mistake?

'I suppose Abigail told you that,' said Oxford. 'I should not be surprised: you have never missed an opportunity to insinuate yourself between me and the Queen. You did exactly the same after I was stabbed, and after my daughter died, and during my recent illness . . . when you see her next, you might advise Lady Masham to look out. She has become no less convinced of her great value to the Queen than her predecessor. She believes that nothing can be achieved unless she has had a part in arranging it. Did you bribe her to supply this private information?'

'If I did, that would hardly be so bad.' Bolingbroke gazed insolently at Oxford. He stood up, grabbing his wig. 'We have done much worse, you and I. We have many German lives on our hands. But we will succeed if our secret is preserved. And if we do succeed, we will have done more service to Britain than all the ministers who went before us. We are disjointed to such a degree that soon nothing will preserve the appearance of our being together,' Bolingbroke said. 'If our enemies sat still for a moment they would see us tear one another to pieces. And we can't afford that. I have always supported you among the Tories but every connection you forge and sustain among the Whigs has threatened my own standing among the Tories.'

With that, Bolingbroke got up and left the room. Oxford waited a short while, then followed ⁄ leaving Defoe alone to get out of the room unobserved.

He could hardly be expected to understand everything he had heard, but nor could he miss the underlying implications. What did Bolingbroke mean, to say they had German lives on their hands? What secrets did they have? And what must Oxford think of Defoe for seeming to spy on him. When he left Stoke Newington this morning, Defoe had planned to amass a vast heap of information by the evening to benefit the Lord Treasurer. But much of what he'd learned actually drove a division between him and his patron. Why had Oxford left the room, instead of waiting to speak to him? Defoe had come to court at great hazard, almost killed a man – perhaps now he had indeed died – got nowhere near the man he had intended to kill, and barged unin⁄ vited into the Lord Treasurer's intimacy. Henceforth, the best he could hope was that Oxford would hold him at a greater distance. At worst, Oxford would turn against him entirely.

'We have many lives on our hands,' said Bolingbroke

Chapter 16

Bring Me my Brandy

It was not easy getting the Queen out of Lady Masham's rooms and back to her own apartments.

For some time, if the Queen wished to travel around the castle she had been taken about in a sedan chair, with not two but four porters to carry her considerable bulk. Unfortunately the door to Lady Masham's room was not wide enough for four men, so they had been obliged to place the sedan on the floor and slide it through. To protect the Queen's dignity, all other traffic through that door was stopped, and servants were instructed to turn away – facing the wall if necessary.

Lady Masham and Mary had followed close behind, Lady Masham having first left instruction that absolutely nobody was to enter her room without her permission. Not even her husband.

When the Queen was back in her own bed, Lady Mary sat beside her for a while, holding her hand, and Lady Masham stayed there too for a while.

'I don't need both of you,' the Queen said. 'Abigail, you have been so very kind. Please get some sleep. And have somebody bring me my brandy.' So Lady Masham left the Queen with Mary.

For some time, neither woman spoke. But Mary could feel the

Queen's hand still squeezing hers, and knew she was not asleep. Suddenly the Queen said, 'It must be very hard for you.'

'Your Majesty, I am very comfortable,' Mary replied.

She realised immediately that the Queen must be talking about something else, but could not guess exactly what it might be. Did she mean the difficulty Mary faced with her father's objections – should he ever find out – to Samuel Holland?

'It must be very hard for you . . .' the Queen was out of breath, exhausted by the sheer effort of speaking her thoughts out loud. 'Hard for you to understand the pain of an old woman who has regrets, and no obvious way to make amends.'

Mary could think of nothing to say, so she squeezed the Queen's hand. Then an idea occurred to her.

'Your Majesty, I would hardly describe you as old.'

'I am not old, it's true. But you see for yourself the condition I am in. When I was young like you I thought I might die of boredom, sitting at tea with old, vapourish women, and playing cards to pass the time. But the end is near. Nobody knows how near it may be, but it can't be long. It may come tomorrow.'

'No, Your Majesty, please . . .'

'But while I live, I know that God has preserved me for some purpose. I just wish I knew what it is.'

She fell silent, and soon afterwards she fell asleep. And Mary slept beside her in her seat.

Chapter 17

A Crushing Sense of Inadequacy

Before leaving, Defoe rifled quickly through Arbuthnot's cup-boards. He soon found what he needed: a riding coat to cover up his borrowed servant's uniform, and a long wig. By now his clothes swap would have been discovered, and any 'servant' with an unfamiliar face would be arrested, and perhaps also charged with murder if the body of Nottingham's man was discovered.

It was the most hazardous moment in Defoe's life. He opened the door nervously. There was nobody in the corridor. He crept quietly towards the end where the light was strongest, at the top of a wide stairway. There was nowhere here to hide. His feet still tingled with pins and needles, so he walked with a slight limp, and would not be able to run if anybody gave chase.

He thought he heard a sound behind him, and turned around fast. A pair of footmen stood near him. They'd been following, but stopped moving when he did.

'What do you want?' Defoe asked.

'We wondered if you might be lost, sir,' said one. He had a weaselly face. Was this a trick?

'I am lost. How do I find my way out?'

'I can show you, sir,' said the other footman. Defoe bowed. He had shoved his pistol in the pocket of Arbuthnot's massive coat, and pushed his hand inside to feel it. There was no way he could get it out and use it. In the same pocket he kept his scarf, for strangling. He doubted he could do that.

A huge sense of dread and failure settled on him. The second footman led him down the stairs and Defoe noted that the other fellow, the weaselly one, had disappeared. Perhaps they trusted him? Or had he gone to fetch reinforcements? And where was this man taking him?

Turning a corner, Defoe recognised the hall where he had glimpsed the Pretender earlier. He pointed to the room he saw him enter and asked the footman whose it was.

'That belongs to Lady Masham, sir.'

'I suppose you want to know why I ask?'

The man looked embarrassed. 'None of my business, sir.'

'Is she in?'

'I could not say, sir. Her Ladyship is frequently elsewhere, attending to Her Majesty. I fear it would be impossible to find out. At this time of night, her Ladyship might be asleep.'

'Of course. I should not be so inquiring. All the same, I am glad to find myself in a place I recognise. You can leave me here, I know my way now.'

'I can't leave you, sir. Only people familiar to the Queen are permitted to stay unaccompanied in this part of the castle . . .'

'What would it take to change your mind?' Defoe had spoken without thinking. He had no money left to bribe the man, and could hardly threaten him.

'I'm sorry, sir . . .'

Defoe felt again the crushing sense of inadequacy to the task he had set himself. He had come here with utterly unrealistic expectations. He thought of the dingy home he had woken in that morning, and the hopelessness of his situation. He must do some-thing – but what? Then he thought of Swift, and of even Pope, sitting at a table sharing jokes with his patron and he was con-sumed with an overwhelming sense of shame and jealousy. Only that morning, Oxford had wanted him to eat with the servants.

Why, after all his hard work, was he not as fortunate as them?

He followed the footmen downstairs, knowing he was walking away from his best chance to find the Pretender and secure some kind of life for his children – even if it was too late for him. To end forever the fear of a Catholic taking the throne again and torturing Defoe's people.

And then something changed his mind. He turned and ran up towards the landing, pulling his pistol from his pocket as he moved, and the powder too. The footman was coming after him but ran silently, mortified, presumably, to have lost control of this intruder. Defoe stopped suddenly and smashed the handle of his pistol into the fellow's forehead. He dropped to the floor almost entirely noiselessly.

Defoe dragged him out of the way, but only to move him towards the wall. There was no time to hide this one, or check his pockets. Glancing occasionally down at him to ensure he had not come to, Defoe poured powder into his pistol and a couple of balls, then breathed deeply before charging into Lady Masham's room.

It was dark inside, and for a moment he could see nothing. He went out again to grab a candle, then back in. He glanced all around.

The bed was empty. Suddenly Defoe remembered what he had not allowed himself to think of – that his family would suffer horribly if he was caught here. His own life was nothing, but as he'd already seen, there was no limit to the cruelty of Nottingham.

He was about to leave when he glimpsed the sleeping figure of a young man, slouched in a chair. Moving closer, Defoe recognised the Pretender, breathing softly. In his hands he clenched a kerchief. His coat hung on the back of the chair, his wig lay on the table beside him.

Here he was. The young man known at court in France as James III of England. The Queen's supposed half-brother. The man who, as a baby, was said to have been smuggled into the birth chamber in a warming pan. How had he been smuggled into the castle now? He'd risked his life to be here, and that risk had misfired. Defoe would kill him now that he had the chance.

But looking at the young man's face in repose, Defoe knew he couldn't do it.

Not asleep, anyway. What if he woke him? Perhaps then he could do it? Maybe. But if he failed? Was there anything else he could do before waking the man?

He felt in his pocket and pulled out the jar of white arsenic. Putting the pistol down quietly, but keeping it close to hand, he tipped a little of the arsenic into a bottle of brandy on the table, and the rest into a glass that stood half-full beside it. For a full minute, he stood swilling the bottle and the glass, to dissolve the odourless, colourless poison. Then he took up his pistol again, walked to the Pretender and shook his shoulder, keeping the pistol pointed directly into his face.

The young man woke quickly, and immediately grasped the threat.

'Are you going to shoot me?'

'Yes . . . I don't know.'

'I think you are afraid.'

'Your father was a tyrant.'

'I am not my father. He was the Queen of England's father too. Will you kill her? I have done you no harm. I don't even know you.'

'Be quiet.'

A sound of women's voices came from the corridor. Defoe had to make a quick decision. If he shot the Pretender, at once he would make life easy for Nonconformists everywhere, and end the hopes of all papists. But he would soon be captured, and never see his family again.

There was another way. He'd used it several times today. He turned the pistol in his hand and smashed it in the Pretender's face, and again and again. The young man put his mouth to his sleeve to muffle his own scream.

'What kind of man are you?' Defoe shouted, frustrated at his own failure. 'Why don't you fight me?' But the Pretender said nothing.

Then as suddenly as he had come in, Defoe ran to the door and left.

In five minutes, he was outside the castle, walking down the high street.

Here he was, the young man known in France as
James III of England

Chapter 18

A Sister, and a Lover Too

There was nobody around, not even a whore. How much the high street had changed since the afternoon!

Defoe was shaking with nervous frustration. He had come to Windsor to look for news of the Pretender, but had never imagined he would actually meet him, far less that he might get the chance to point a pistol in the man's face. The significance of what he might have done was enormous, but he felt too a strong sense of failure – he had let the man live. Striking him with the pistol had been the act of a coward, a useless attempt to make up for an unwillingness to kill him outright. The evening had been a total disaster. He had probably killed a man, injured another, spent what little money he had, and been caught spying on his own patron. He felt sick, and suddenly, uncontrollably, he vomited. It splashed back on his feet and legs.

For a long time he stood there, bent in half, his mind racing.

When his breathing had returned to normal, he stood up again. But his mind was still racing. He told himself to stop, to pray, to wait for the voice of God – but he couldn't do it. He felt himself consumed in the flames of hell, but they didn't hurt. They warmed him. The devil had taken him, and he didn't care.

Perhaps all was not lost! Oxford would be glad to hear news of the Pretender — perhaps if Defoe could find the Lord Treasurer he might have the man arrested. But Defoe wanted more. He needed to get rid of this dreadful sense of frustration. He decided to settle a score with Swift and Pope.

Reaching the lodgings of Mrs Partridge, Defoe looked for an open window and soon found one at the side of the house. Climbing in silently, he found himself in a bedroom.

A woman lay snoring on a couch. She had a large bunch of keys in her hand. This must be Mrs Partridge.

Defoe crept through her room and into the hallway, near the front door. He cast his eye around the painting and gilding, the fine shelves and shutters, glass doors, sash windows, branched candlesticks and other furnishings that made the lodgings seem more like a toy shop, or pastry cook's shop.

To the back, he guessed he would find only the kitchen and servants' quarters. Opening the door opposite, he found the dining room. He started up the stairs. The best rooms would be at the front. He tried one, lifting the latch as quietly as he could, and saw a room with two beds. In one lay the unmistakably small figure of Pope. In the other, harder to recognise without his wig, lay Swift.

What to do?

He cursed himself for using all the arsenic. If he'd kept a little, he could have administered a salutary vomiting session to Swift and Pope.

He took the jester's cap out of his own pocket and shoved it into Swift's coat, along with Nelson's Guide.

Then remembering the thread he'd taken from the footman, Defoe crept towards Swift and wrapped it over him and under the bed, a loose spider's web. He took a lock of the man's hair and tied it to the thread, then tied that to the metal bedstead. He expected Swift to wake, but he didn't, so Defoe did the same again, tying more and more of his hair down. It might not hold, but Swift would feel great pain if he tried sitting up.

The work was calming, but if anything it only increased Defoe's cold fury. When he'd run out of thread, he placed a hand over Swift's mouth and nose – waking him at once.

'Keep quiet, or I will kill you,' he whispered, pointing his pistol at Swift and gesturing with his other hand at Pope.

Swift tried to nod, but flinched at even that small movement.

'And keep still, or you will pull the hairs off your head.'

Defoe took his hand off Swift's mouth.

'What do you want?' Swift whispered.

'What is your hold over the Lord Treasurer?'

'I have no hold over him.'

'You're lying.' Defoe tapped roughly on Swift's throat with the pistol. 'Tell me.'

'I have nothing. He likes me. He likes writers. He is generous to writers. He asked me to write for him, and I did so.'

'Not everybody who writes for him dines with the Lord Treasurer inside the castle, or dares to speak to him so forwardly. Why you? Why should he like you?'

'I don't know! I make him laugh? I work hard for him?' Swift paused. He knew the intruder was not satisfied. 'I put my own life in danger, once, opening a bomb that was addressed to him.'

'And you would milk him forever after?'

'I only want what any man might ask for – a secure living that is well within his Lordship's means.'

'There is nobody as grasping as a parson,' said Defoe. He was enjoying himself.

'Are you working for his Lordship?'

'I am.'

'I only ask him to help me to a better life than I had in Ireland. Is that so bad? The Lord Treasurer is a fine fellow, and . . .'

Defoe flicked a finger in Swift's eye. Swift flinched, started to blink furiously, tears rolling down his cheek.

'Tell me about Ireland. Who is your mistress there?'

'I have no mistress there.'

'Liar. The time of mercy is past. Your day of grace is over.'

'Oh, please! I have a friend. I call her Stella.'

'Stella? Is she your lover? Is she?' He flicked Swift's other eye. The tears ran down faster than before as Swift blinked furiously. But he said nothing.

'Is she your lover? Tell me, or I'll cut your bollocks off.' He had no knife, but Swift didn't know that.

'Yes! Is that what you want me to say?'

Defoe was annoyed. Had Swift admitted it or not?

'What about Hester Vanhomrigh? When does she fit into your busy schedule, Parson?'

'Who are you? Why do you ask me this?'

'Who is Stella? Is she rich?'

'No, she has nothing. She's my sister. There, I have said it. Pray God my friend Pope is still sleeping.' Swift was weeping copiously, and not only because Defoe had flicked his eyes.

'Your lover and your sister too? Is that normal in the Church of England?'

'She doesn't know that I am her brother. We are only half siblings. Our natural father was Sir William Temple. A great man, whom I worshipped when he lived. I was his secretary.

Nobody knew I was his natural son, and I was forbidden to join the family at meal times.'

Defoe asked how Swift could be sure he was Temple's son.

'I only learned I was his son when he was dying. He gave me money, and his memoirs to publish. He gave me proof my supposed father was not in the right place at the time of my conception. Stella was another of his natural children. I tutored her.'

'Temple should have eaten his babies sooner than let them be such a burden on the world. And you should be ashamed. You must choose one woman – a woman you are not related to – and marry her.'

'I am in no position to marry. Please tell his Lordship. I am sorry if I went too far. I had no idea. I do it all the time. I am sorry. Truly sorry. But please don't tell him about my . . . friends. They are both special to me, but he may not understand. The Queen will not approve, and she already dislikes me. If she takes against me, I shall never get the living I want. Please, Your Honour, let me give you all I have. It's not much, but I beg you . . .'

'I will take it. But I make no promises . . . and tell me, where does the little papist keep his money?'

'Under his bed.' Swift went quiet, listening for the sound of Pope's breathing. He could hear nothing. 'Dear friend, if you are awake, forgive me.'

Defoe reached under Pope's bed and rummaged through his bags. There were ninety guineas. Defoe took them. Then he caught sight of quills and ink on a dresser. In his savage mood, he was tempted to crush the pens, and pour ink over Swift. But to someone who has little, such a gesture could only seem extravagant.

Instead, he put the ink in his pocket and thrust the pens savagely towards Swift's face, before putting them, too, in his pocket.

And then he left.

'I only want what any man might ask for,' said Swift.
'A secure living.'

Chapter 19

Does God Love You, Daniel?

When Defoe got back to his own lodgings, it was almost dawn. He had been awake for more than twenty-four hours. He had a surprise: his wife was waiting for him on the front doorstep.

'Daniel,' Sarah said. 'Where have you been?'

'My sweet! What are you doing here?'

She had followed him to Windsor, accompanied by their eldest son, who slept inside now. They had travelled on horses they borrowed from God-fearing neighbours. They had found the inn because they chanced to see his horse there.

'I had not expected you to stay away so long,' she said. 'What has happened to you? Did you speak to the Lord Treasurer?'

'I did.'

'You have a new coat. Where is your old one?'

'I had to leave it in the castle.'

'Daniel, have you been whoring?'

She had never asked him anything like this before. Until now, she had trusted him in every way. He bitterly regretted that she had found him with the sword, and pistol. How could he win her trust again?

'My love, I have never been whoring. All that I have done,

165

when I have done it without telling you, has been for your sake or the sake of our children, as God loves me.'

'Does God love you, Daniel? Please tell me what you have done.'

After years of secrecy, it went against all his instincts to tell her the truth. 'I have done nothing wrong. How can you suspect me?'

She said nothing, but her expression changed from concern to something more like disgust. 'I don't believe you. Like a fool, I have trusted you for too long. Now I know you are lying.'

He thought he might be able to give her an account that left out the worst of what had passed, but one thing led directly to the next, and in a sudden outpouring he told her everything. 'I am ashamed. I have failed you. I have deceived myself, and the best of women. I have puffed myself up with pride, and the Lord has abandoned me.'

He felt empty. But a huge burden lifted from his shoulders as he spoke to her truthfully at last. He told her about his disappointing conversation with Oxford, described accidentally killing one man, failing to kill another, and cruelly torturing Swift. As he spoke, he shed hot tears of frustration and shame.

She put her arms around him. He rested his head on her shoulder, heaving gently with exhaustion and hunger.

At last, she spoke. 'Daniel, your life is in danger. If you are recognised by the footman who fainted, or the one who lent you his livery, or the one who tried to escort you from the castle, you could be hanged.'

'I know.'

'But if you can help to have the Pretender arrested you may throw yourself on the mercy of the Queen.'

'I can't go back! I'll be killed. Can't you take a message to Oxford for me?' he asked in despair. 'Or the boy?'

Once before, when he was on the run from Nottingham, Defoe had sent his son to Oxford for help. Why not again?

'There is no way we could get access to him. Only you know how to do that. And there is no time to waste. You must tell him about the Pretender and what you learned about Swift. That alone might be worth some reward. This gives him a reason to put an end to Swift's begging for preferment.'

'He's hardly going to look favourably on me after I have been caught spying on him.'

'That is unfortunate. But you have worked tirelessly on his behalf. It pains me to hear how slavishly you profess yourself his servant. He can't possibly believe you intended to spy on him.'

'It's hardly to my credit as a spy if I don't know my master's friends.'

'The Lord Treasurer is notoriously secretive. If you have a fault, it's your affection and loyalty towards those who treat you with kindness – precisely the qualities that steered you away from prying too closely into his affairs. You made a mistake, but a forgivable one. Tell him about Swift and he'll thank you. Now, tell me again what you know . . .'

'When Swift was a young man his patron was Sir William Temple. Temple left him money when he died, and certain memoirs to publish, which earned him more. I remember when they appeared they upset several people still alive, including the Queen's friend the Duchess of Somerset . . . tonight I have spoken with Swift's mistress Hester Vanhomrigh – she's here in London. He told me he had another mistress in Dublin, called Stella, who is his natural sister. They met at Temple's house when she was just a girl.'

'And he knows she's his sister?'

'He told me that, but I can't prove it.'

'You must pass on this information. But do it out of Christian charity, not jealousy of a man more successful than yourself.'

Sarah had always supported Defoe's projects, no matter how outlandish

Chapter 20

Sharing an Apple

Early the next morning, after Lady Masham arrived in the Queen's chambers, Mary asked to be excused.

She went out into the gardens. She could only hope he waited for her.

She found him in the walled garden, leaning beside an apple tree trained against a wall. How lovely he looked, his smile bursting across his face at the sight of her! But they dared not to be seen together, not even by the gardeners digging nearby, lest word should get back to her father.

Samuel pulled an apple from the tree and turned to walk through a gate. Outside the walled garden was a terrace, with a raised level overlooking an enclosure with a shallow pond. On each side of the pond were benches. Samuel sat on one bench and Mary went to sit on another.

He started to polish the apple on his coat, then placed it with some ceremony on the bench beside him. On top of it he placed a clean kerchief, like a conjuror at the Smithfield fair. And then he walked away to another bench.

Mary got up and moved to the bench with the apple. She removed the cloth and polished the apple on one of her petticoats, then she kissed it and replaced it — on top of the kerchief this time — and returned to the bench where she had sat before.

Samuel looked around to make sure they were not being watched, then returned to the apple and kissed it. He clasped it in both hands, as careful and tender as if it were Mary's hand.

'We must not merely touch it, dearest,' Mary said, just loud enough to be heard. 'You must take a bite. But leave some for me.'

Samuel bit the apple. It was a juicy one, and sweeter than he could have expected this early in the summer. He was about to put it back on the kerchief, but a fit of boldness swept through him and he carried it to Mary instead. He held it before her mouth and she took a bite. The juice ran on her lip and Samuel gently dabbed her mouth with his kerchief.

'My darling,' she said. 'I will burst if I don't tell my father soon. One of these days he might open one of your letters. If he found out that way, he would absolutely forbid me to marry you. Can I tell him? Trust his better nature to make the right decision?'

'We must wait a little longer.'

'It kills me to deceive him,' Mary said.

'I know, but we must. Last night before the ball my groom had occasion to whip another servant who spoke to him vilely. I went to intervene and found myself facing your father. It seems the rude fellow was his footman.'

Mary looked appalled. 'What happened?'

'Your father struck my man with his whip. For a moment it looked as if his Lordship was going to challenge me. But I bowed as low as I could without falling on my face and he turned away.'

'Oh no. This is terrible news.'

'You have told me often enough that he will not allow you to marry somebody whose family helped to send King James into exile.' As one of several prominent Whigs, Samuel's father had signed an invitation to William of Orange to invade England. King James fled, and was deemed to have abdicated. 'After last night,' Samuel continued, 'nothing could recommend me to him.'

'Well, he loves me and trusts me and he knows I would not throw myself away on just anybody.'

'When we first met, my darling, you were just a girl. He didn't mind, then, if you talked to Whig children at church. But now you are transformed. Naturally your father hopes you will do better than marry me.'

'He's not the bigot you take him for.'

'I don't believe he's a bigot. I have admired him. But consider how events have taught him to distrust Whigs. He was a witness to the birth of the so-called Pretender. He saw it with his own eyes. To him above all people, the idea that some foundling was smuggled into the chamber in a warming pan, before all those witnesses, defies all credibility. But that's the story people chose to believe.'

Mary looked around again to see if they might be watched.

'It's shameful,' Samuel continued. 'If only Queen Anne had been present too she would have known the prince was truly her brother.'

'My love, it may be treason to say this, but she took care to be absent,' said Mary. 'She chose to believe the false stories. I heard her say so last night. She would never have been Queen if her brother were recognised as legitimate.'

Samuel paused. 'I love her, because you tell me I must, but what she did as a young woman is hard to understand. And it's because of when happened to King James and his son that your father felt obliged to renounce Rome.'

Mary seized his hand.

'He did it for me! It was impossible to continue living as he wished unless he publicly embraced the Church of England.'

Samuel detached his hand, but sat down beside her.

'The Church of Rome promises eternal damnation for apostates. Your father walks on a thin crust of earth that might open up and swallow him in flames at any time. He knows your mother would never have approved. Their parents, and grandparents, endured terrible persecution. How could he turn his back on so much suffering? If he didn't honour his own father and mother, how could he expect his own children to honour him? These are the things that distress your father. If you marry me, the betrayal of your Roman Catholic forebears — as he sees it — would be irreversible.'

'But that will never change,' said Mary. 'So what are we waiting for?'

'If the Pretender succeeds, as by right I accept he should, your father may go back to Rome. Perhaps then he'll be more forgiving. He may even try to convert me,' said Samuel.

But how could they be sure the Pretender would succeed?

'Naturally your father hopes you will do better than marry me,' said Samuel

Chapter 21

A New Species of Writing

Defoe had hardly slept but he knew he must get to Lord Oxford as early as possible. He sent his son ahead with a sealed letter to deliver to the castle. This told Oxford that Defoe had news of the greatest possible importance, and needed to speak privately with him. Now Defoe would just have to take his chances and hope that nobody recognised him – that Oxford didn't have him thrown out, or arrested for treason and murder.

By prior arrangement, Defoe met his son at a tavern on the outer edge of Windsor. The boy had a reply from Oxford: Come at once, before my levee starts.

Defoe hastened to the castle on the horse his son had ridden the previous day. He wore a wide hat, pulled low over his face, and said little as he gave the horse to the Queen's stablemen.

He walked inside the castle, pausing briefly to ask for directions. A thought crossed his mind: had Sarah sent him here to die? Perhaps she hated him, now that she knew him to be a liar and, much worse, a murderer. And her life might not be significantly worse without him. If she cast up her account, these items would weigh sorrily in his profit and loss, and it would take many years to recover his good husbandry – if by God's grace he had many years left.

Feeling utterly alone, Defoe hardly cared if he lived or died. But to be executed would be horrible: he couldn't bear to think of his children learning that he had died violently. He must do all he could to survive, and let Sarah keep him if she would.

With every glance from the liveried servants, Defoe felt his heart race, but nobody attempted to stop him. When he reached the rooms that he had been told to go to, he gave his real name, and a servant walked him inside then closed the door behind him. He was alone with Oxford.

Getting straight to the point, Defoe told Oxford that he had seen the Pretender, here in the castle. He was going into the rooms of Lady Masham. If the Lord Treasurer were to send somebody there now, they might catch him.

'I can't do that, Daniel. If they find nobody there, I will probably lose my white staff. But I can speak to the captain of the guard about this, and ask him to be especially vigilant. Would you like to describe him? I can call the captain . . .'

'I would rather tell you, my lord.'

Defoe gave the best description he could manage, mentioning the bruised face. After a long silence, Oxford spoke.

'You have done well, Daniel. But I fear that I still don't have any funds to pay you . . .'

It hurt to hear this, but Defoe had expected it, and he still felt intense loyalty to his patron. After what had passed with Sarah, it might be that Oxford was the only person alive who still respected him.

'My lord, before I leave, permit me to speak freely. I believe your position is at risk and you are not doing enough to secure it.'

'None of us can be sure what the future holds. You must make plans.'

'I do, my lord. I do.'

'Oh really? What are they?' Oxford added. He sounded genu-inely curious, but Defoe hesitated.

'I'm embarrassed to tell you.'

'Don't be.'

'My best hope is to continue working with you, my lord.' Defoe paused. Oxford looked mildly irritated. But still Defoe hardly dared to describe his idea. 'If that must end, I must rely on my pen. I plan to introduce a new species of writing that will do without the improbable and marvellous. I will use prose instead of verse, because rhymes are stubborn things while prose can be written as fast as you set pen to paper. Anyway a naked, natural way of speaking is the only thing to draw in readers. Once they start my stories, they'll find it hard to get out until they finish.'

'I hope you're right.'

'You don't believe it. You're right. It's madness.' He slumped, feeling defeated again.

'Daniel, I love books as much as any man. My collection is one of the largest in the country. But I doubt you will earn sufficient money to support a large family. Only poetry will do that. Look at the success of Pope's latest.'

Having been crushed only moments before, Defoe felt his pride revive at the mention of Pope's name. 'My lord, the potential market for my books is huge. Mr Addison claims to sell forty-five thousand copies of his *Spectator* each week, and he says each copy is seen by twenty people. That amounts to 900,000 readers. Of those, I believe I can attract a substantial portion if my books are presented attractively. At five shillings a copy they'd be out of the reach of tinkers and coal heavers, but shopkeepers might afford them . . . I could surely sell more than the fashionable poets, with their verse epics, richly bound, priced at several guineas a set.'

'Have you chosen a story?' Oxford asked.

'I have chosen many stories. I shall write the first very quickly – in weeks – about that fellow that was washed ashore on an island full of savages.'

'A satire?' Oxford looked unconvinced. 'I wish you luck. Swift, as it happens, has a similar idea.'

Defoe looked appalled. 'My lord, when I was young I always loved reading, and I dreamed of writing. At school I experimented by borrowing from the great writers of the past. But I would never copy Swift.'

Oxford nodded.

'That's not all, my lord . . .'

He told Oxford what he knew about Swift's incestuous relationship – though naturally he gave no hint at how he had come by the information.

'I'm sorry,' he concluded. 'I know that Dr Swift has served you well. But he does not seem the right sort to be made a bishop in the Church of England.'

'I am fond of him. He saved my life once. At great personal risk to himself.'

Defoe nodded. There was a long silence before Oxford spoke again.

'In the meantime, I shall do my best for you. I have considered your suggestion and determined to pay handsomely for the information you have given. I think I might be able to find five thousand pounds to pay off your outstanding debts. That was the amount, was it not?'

'Five thousand!'

Defoe could hardly begin to understand why Oxford was doing this. Only moments before, he had said there were no funds. But in his darkest moment, in his despair, God had chosen to forgive him, and to use Oxford as his messenger. Defoe fell to his knees and clutched Oxford's feet.

Oxford smiled, and urged him to rise.

'Come back to the castle this afternoon and I'll give you the money directly. But be sure to bring with you the evidence you have gathered regarding Dr Swift's birth, and that of his mistress. I want every scrap. And bring anything you have on Bolingbroke, and any other man or woman you suspect may be involved with the Pretender.'

Defoe felt desperate again. He had no certain evidence. But perhaps there was still time. 'Thank you. But, my lord, please only help me because you value the information I bring. Don't pay because I . . . happened to overhear your conversation with the Secretary of State.'

Oxford looked grave, but said nothing.

Chapter 22

Losing Confidence in Oxford

Later that morning, the Queen held a meeting of her chief ministers in her bedroom. She lay in bed, with Lady Masham sitting beside her. The ministers stood at the foot of the bed. The Queen was feeling tired, so most of the business they hoped to discuss had to be put off till later. But before leaving the room Oxford said, 'Your Majesty, there is one small matter. I beg you to allow me once more to recommend Dr Swift for the next vacancy as bishop. He has served the administration with considerable energy.'

To everyone's surprise, Bolingbroke agreed. 'Swift has been a loyal supporter, Your Majesty.'

But Oxford had not chosen a good moment. 'It brings me joy to see you in agreement, but I am not an admirer of Dr Swift,' the Queen said.

'He has no principles,' added the Duchess of Somerset.

'You may ask me another time,' said the Queen. 'But not today. Now if you will forgive me I need some rest.'

The ministers bowed and moved towards the door. On the way out, Oxford caught the eye of Lady Masham, and beckoned her to follow. Mary saw it, and she saw Bolingbroke notice it too. Oxford was last of the ministers to leave the room, and Lady

Masham followed him to the door, near where Mary was standing. The Queen was talking in a low voice to the Duchess, so Mary stepped closer to the door in hope she might overhear Oxford. She had become quite a spy.

She missed the start of the conversation. The first voice she heard, whispering angrily, was Lady Masham's.

'Why should I help you? You did nothing for me, paid no notice of me until the Queen showed me favour . . .'

'Dear cousin,' said Oxford. 'I ask only for a short-term loan. You cannot refuse me?'

'It's impossible. What makes you think I have that kind of sum?'

Oxford's whispering had been bland and polite. Now he spoke as fiercely as her. 'I know it for a fact,' he hissed. 'You must give me what I need.'

Not wishing to be caught eavesdropping, Mary withdrew towards the Queen's bed, and therefore missed the outcome of this bad-tempered exchange. Lady Masham returned to the room looking entirely normal, all trace of ill-temper wiped from her face. She sent for some food for the Queen's luncheon.

'I am really not hungry yet, dear Abigail.'

The Duchess proposed a few hands at whist, and went herself to fetch the cards from a box at the far end of the room. While she was doing that, the Queen said:

'Abigail, I am losing confidence in Oxford. Can I trust him?'

'Your Majesty, I hesitate to pass judgement on my own dear cousin but your suspicions match my own. He tells lies, and I'm persuaded that he is stealing money.'

'God forgive him,' said the Queen, evidently shocked.

Mary was appalled that Lady Masham could say such bare-faced lies. But she said nothing.

After a moment, Lady Masham spoke. 'The Earl of Boling-broke is honest.'

'But he is not so regular in his private life as he ought to be,' the Queen replied. 'His wife bores him, and he treats her inexcusably. The Duchess tells me he runs after street whores and barmaids.'

Mary watched to see if Lady Masham would look at the Duchess, but they both studied their cards.

'I find that hard to believe, Your Majesty,' said Lady Masham.

The food arrived on a wheeled trolley. There was bread and cheese and cold beef. But the Queen said she was not hungry; so they carried on playing cards until the Queen remembered that the others might like to eat. They affected not to be hungry but she insisted. Soon the three of them were sitting around a table, eating as fast as became them.

Lady Masham called for some tea. When it arrived, she let her own dish get cold and then Mary was astonished to see her pour it over her own dress, and affect to have done it as an accident.

'Your Majesty, I beg you to forgive me but I must leave you briefly.'

The Queen had not seen her spill the tea.

'You are constantly disappearing, Abigail. What can possibly be so important when I need you here?'

Lady Masham walked in front of her, showing the stain on her dress. The Queen smiled and said of course she must go.

She was gone for a long time, but she was not missed because the Queen dozed, and Mary became quite involved in a conversa-tion with the Duchess about Samuel. The Duchess had always married for convenience, not for love, and seemed fascinated by

Samuel's poetical wooing. She asked if Mary had any of his poems that she might look at, and Mary shyly handed over the poem Samuel had sent the day before. The Duchess read it out loud, which made Mary blush with pleasure and embarrassment together.

'I do hope you find a way to bring your father around to him,' said the Duchess. 'Have you thought of asking the Queen to speak for you?'

The Queen woke soon after, and the luncheon was taken away. 'Is Abigail away all this time?' the Queen asked.

'Would you like me to fetch her?' Mary offered, rising from her chair.

'No, there is no need. Thank you.' After a moment, the Queen said, 'What about you, Mary? What do you think of Oxford?'

'I hope I would speak out, regardless of his eminence, if I knew he had done wrong. But that's more than I know.'

'And Bolingbroke?'

Mary hesitated. 'I can't say I am surprised by what you have heard.'

The Queen smiled. 'Abigail is too good. She always thinks the best of people.'

The Duchess snorted, but the Queen didn't hear her. Then the Duchess changed the subject.

'Your Majesty, we were talking while you slept about Mary's sweetheart, Samuel Holland. Mary showed me one of the poems he has written for her.'

'Tell me,' the Queen said to Mary, 'have you told your father about him?'

It was now or never. 'I daren't, Your Majesty. Perhaps you might be good enough to speak to him for me?'

183

The Queen did not answer immediately, and Mary realised with shame that she had joined the line of people hoping the Queen might do something for them before it was too late. It seemed that she, too, was to be disappointed.

'No, I don't think that would do,' the Queen said. 'You must put your trust in God.'

'I do, Your Majesty.' Mary curtsied.

*

The clock had just chimed three when Lady Masham returned, preceded by a muffled commotion outside. 'Your Majesty,' she said with a smile, 'I have prepared a surprise for you. I beg you to come and see it.'

'Thank you, Abigail. But can't you bring it here?'

'It might not survive the journey. You must come down to the rose garden.'

'I can't possibly.'

'I beg you, Majesty, to allow this one excursion. I would not ask if I did not truly believe, with all my heart, that it might make you very happy.'

She opened the door, revealing four footmen and the Queen's sedan chair. 'I have taken the liberty of preparing a conveyance.'

Chapter 23

Forgive Me

Reluctantly, the Queen allowed herself to be manoeuvred into the sedan and carried downstairs towards the garden.

Lady Masham had icily informed the Duchess that she was unlikely to take much pleasure in the surprise. But the Duchess had already decided not to ask about it or show any interest. She would stay where she was, thank you. The Queen, having some idea how little the two women liked each other, was willing to leave her – but insisted on Mary's coming. Lady Masham looked annoyed but didn't argue.

On the way downstairs, Lady Masham walked beside the sedan, speaking into the window which the Queen left open for fresh air. And she spoke in a tone of sweetness and tenderness that Mary, at any rate, had never heard from her before.

'Your Majesty, I pray that you will accept this surprise as an expression of the great love I have for you, and gratitude for all you have done for me. When I came to court, I was nothing, and I expected to stay nothing.'

'Abigail . . .' The Queen was obviously struck, too, by Lady Masham's unwonted tone.

'Please, Your Majesty,' Lady Masham continued. 'I have known poverty, but I always determined to work hard, knowing that if I did I might be able to provide better for my children. When Sarah Churchill left you – the Duchess of Marlborough, I should say – I never imagined that you would bestow your favour on me, or that you would elevate my dear husband to the Lords. I will always be thankful . . .'

'Abigail, I am so happy to hear this. I have done what I could for you, but I always feared losing you if I elevated you too high. I worried that perhaps you were cross with me for making Samuel a mere baron. What you say gives me more pleasure than you can imagine . . . I will always love you, Abigail.'

Lady Masham put her hand through the window of the sedan and the Queen took hold of it. Mary walked behind, seemingly forgotten by all.

In the garden, Lady Masham instructed the footmen to put down the Queen's sedan and come with her to fetch the surprise from inside the castle.

'But you said it was in the garden . . .?' the Queen said.

'Your Majesty, it is too precious to be left unattended. Please give me five minutes. You see that Mary is here to keep you company.'

'Well then I shall wait,' said the Queen. 'But when you come back, bring me some brandy.'

Lady Masham promised to do so and left in a hurry, the footmen running behind her to keep up.

Mary asked if the Queen would care to step out of the sedan and move to a bench – the same bench where Mary had sat with Samuel only hours earlier. But the Queen had judged it might not be sensible with only Mary around to help.

So they sat with the door open, listening to magpies bickering in a nearby oak.

Soon enough, Lady Masham dashed into the private area where they sat, largely hidden from the view of prying eyes.

'Here it comes, Your Majesty!' And she waved behind her to a space in the wall that was presently filled with another sedan chair, carried by the same tired-looking footmen.

'Set it down just here,' said Lady Masham, indicating a space just beside the door of the Queen's sedan.

'That's right. Now go back into the castle and make sure that we are undisturbed. I don't want to see anyone. I will come and find you when we need you again.'

The footmen walked backwards towards the gap in the wall, bowed, then turned towards the palace.

'Your Majesty,' said Lady Masham, putting the unfinished brandy bottle she had found in her room, and a glass, into the Queen's hands. 'Permit me to show you your surprise.'

The door of the Queen's sedan stood wide open. Her Majesty leaned out as much as she could comfortably manage.

Lady Masham walked to the door of the other sedan and opened it with a flourish – revealing a young man with a bruise around his left eye.

Perhaps surprisingly, the Queen recognised him at once. Her mouth fell open.

'My father's ghost? That face. Those hands.'

Without stepping outside the sedan, the young man got down on his knees. 'Sister, I would kiss your hand but I dare not show myself.'

'This is a shock,' said the Queen. "I will not listen. Take me back. Take me back!'

Lady Masham didn't move.

'You carry me here as if I have no choice,' the Queen said. 'I command you to take me back.'

'I bring a message from the best of men,' the Pretender said. 'Before his death, our father bid me find means to let you know that he forgave you from the bottom of his heart, and prayed God to do so too.'

'He killed all my children – his curse. Forgiveness will not bring them back.'

Mary hardly knew where to look. So this was James Stuart, the man who called himself James the Third, her father's great hope for the succession. She was amazed to see him here. But what had happened to him? Why was he bruised?

'Dear sister, he knew how you suffered. When we heard of the death of your little ones we were moved to tears. Our father spoke often of how he used to play with you, and with our dearly missed sister Mary, when you were little girls together. He knew that you took care to absent yourself from my birth, and that you declined to speak up for me when people gossiped – but he gave you his last blessing, and prayed that you might convert your heart, and find the resolution to repair to his son the wrongs you did to him.' He paused. 'I pray you, don't hate me for not being your own son.'

The Queen got off her seat and joined him on her knees. Tears ran down her face. She clasped her hands in prayer and turned them towards Lady Masham. 'Please, Abigail, take me inside.'

'I can never abandon my kingdom,' the prince continued, 'but I would rather owe to you than to any living person, the recovery of it.'

Lady Masham went over to the Queen, knelt and took her hands. 'Your Majesty, the Prince has taken a terrible risk coming here. He knows there is a price on his head.'

The Queen seemed not to hear. She stared at her brother, but seemed to see through him, her eyes closed as she remembered something long before.

'You were just a baby.'

'The Prince and your father were hurried abroad, in dead of darkness,' Lady Masham said, 'and abandoned several leagues at sea.'

'Madam,' said the Pretender, 'I love you because my father and mother taught me I should love you.'

'Ha!' The Queen could not believe it.

'He forgave you and wished he could undo the wrong he did you.'

'What wrong did he do?'

'The curse he sent you, that killed your children, I remember the day he wrote it, he was in a terrible rage, screaming and cursing at my mother, the sweetest, most devout . . . and at me, he cursed me for a disappointment. I disgusted him because his sorrows started when I was born, and he wanted me to be perfect, and I never was perfect, Madam, and I hated you for what you did to us. But my mother was kind, and gentle, and she taught me to remember the good example of our Saviour, and she taught our father too, kneeling before him until he saw her pure love and his heart softened. And no sooner had he sent the letter to you did he start to regret it, weeping, and crying out about you. "Does she ever think of me?" he asked. And he told us stories about how he would play with you when you were but a little girl. He wept that he'd sent such a curse to you, and killed his own grandchildren, and I know exactly what he wrote because I was there when he wrote it, shouting it aloud, though I pretended not to listen, pretended to be interested only in my food, and he blamed me for that, too, for eating too much. When we first heard of your children's deaths I rejoiced. It shames me to say it, but that's the truth. But I saw my mother crying at the news and my father too, and I felt ashamed, and from that time onwards I shed tears with them.'

He paused, but the Queen said nothing, so he continued. 'Sister, I have written to you many times, and heard nothing from you, but let us be friends.'

'When I received that letter,' the Queen said, 'I felt as if the blood had spilled from a great hole in my heart, and washed all over the floor around me.'

'Did your husband help you?'

'I told him nothing. It was my own hidden evil that had caused this. But he guessed what the letter said. He guessed, but said nothing. He could never hear a disagreeable word but must always shift away, walking cheerfully about a room as if he were wandering in the park. He was useless to me. I never felt so alone.'

'Sister . . .'

'Forgive me,' said the Queen. At first, the Pretender thought she meant only to apologise for interrupting him, but she said it again. 'Forgive me.'

'I shall, I do,' he replied. 'Your own good nature, sister, and your natural affection to a brother from whom you never received any injury, cannot but incline your heart to do him justice. And as it is in your power, I cannot doubt your good inclinations.'

There was a long period of silence. The Queen stared at her brother and felt nothing but love for him. After several minutes, he said: 'I know that you have no love for the German Elector, who refused your hand when he had the chance.'

'Your mother would have forgiven him,' Anne said. 'But I'm

not as good as her. I don't think I can. When I was younger than you are now, I was told a man had come from overseas to ask for my hand, and when he came to see me I resolved to flirt, and tease him. I had no great love for him, he was a German, and spoke little English, with a strong accent, and he had (or my mind deceives me) a great deformity, though I cannot remember now if it was his leg, or an arm – but no matter. And so we teased him, and my dear friend Sarah – my former friend Sarah – hid his hat after he put it down and we laughed as he paced about, saying he had come to speak with me about a matter of great importance. And of course I had it already from our father what the important matter was that he wanted to speak of with me, but I was minded to make it difficult for him. I had no great desire to live in Hano-ver, but I was not thinking of the future, only of the joy I naturally felt that a man had travelled so far to ask for me. For you know, I was a plain girl, large of stature and with a squint. But I was a fool for my goings-on misfired, and suddenly after much pacing he said he had come to ask for my hand but "you don't please me", he said. And at once I started to burn with shame. I would never know what displeased him, my manners or my looks, but in my shame I forgot at once to play the coquette and I begged him to reconsider. It would be the end of me, I told him. Do not aban-don me! Just think what my father will say, and the court! But he didn't care, and said that with my permission he would go hunt-ing now, and I gave him permission and he started to leave and I sobbed and sobbed, thinking he had gone, but all that time he stood there watching me, for he could not find his hat and Sarah was too worried about me to fetch it for him from where she had hidden it.'

The Pretender said nothing, but smiled sadly. Then a long

period passed in which nobody spoke a word. Then the Queen took a deep breath and said: 'The Act of Settlement was framed to keep Catholics off the throne. You have never offered to change your faith.'

'Laws can be changed,' he replied. 'Once I take possession of what is rightly mine.'

'I would like to make things right. I really want to. There is so much to do. Abigail, please take my brother back to where he is safe, then bring me back inside. And please, fetch me some paper and ink. I think I have finally understood why the Lord preserved me for so long.'

George of Hanover had come to England to ask for Anne's hand.
But she didn't please him

Chapter 24

The Happy News Spreads

Only later, after the Queen had died, did Mary learn what Lady Masham did next, and how the few words she uttered inside the castle would spread, like fire on dry straw, throughout the court and perhaps beyond.

Having first gone inside to fetch the footmen, Lady Masham accompanied them to the garden to fetch the Prince's sedan chair, the windows all closed up for privacy, and carry him back to her rooms. There she gave strict instructions that nobody was to come – not even her husband – and she stayed in the rooms for quite some time after, searching high and low, one imagines, for the requested paper and pen.

One small incident occurred on the journey from the garden to Lady Masham's apartment – an incident so minor that Lady Masham may not have realised what she had done. Happening to pass a certain Catholic gentleman, she broke away from the sedan for a moment to tell him, out of sheer excitement, that she had it on the very best authority that the Queen was preparing to name the Pretender as her successor. And having casually delivered this astonishing news, she hurried after the sedan on its way upstairs.

Within minutes, the Catholic gentleman had passed on the happy news to other Catholic gentlemen, and to no few Anglicans

too. And in no time those others passed it on, adding as confirma-
tion the fact that it came from none other than Lady Masham as
she accompanied the Queen's sedan through the castle.

The result was that within less than half an hour of the
Queen's unexpected interview with her brother, people who had
hitherto avoided showing any clear preference in the matter of the
succession started to announce themselves as having supported the
cause of the Pretender all along. Some even flourished letters they
had received from the Pretender, thanking them for their support
and, in several cases, offering explicit promises of position when
he came into what was rightfully his.

One who was happy to let his true feelings be known was
Alexander Pope, who heard the news from Arbuthnot, when the
doctor came rushing into the room. Pope was transformed, no
longer circumspect but effusive.

'My dear friends,' he said. 'Having always taken care to defend
myself against the danger of criticism for my faith, I have bitten
my tongue when others made slighting remarks. But you, dear
friends, have shown me nothing but kindness. I have in my pocket
a letter from James Stuart, whom I would call James III, were it
not for my duty to the present Queen, while she lives. He assures
me that I shall immediately be granted the position of Poet Laureate when he becomes King.'

'Congratulations, my dear Pope,' said Parnell. 'You deserve it.
I only hope you will remember your old friends then.'

Pope promised he would certainly do that. He told them he
looked forward to the day when Catholics were allowed again
to own property in central London. He had had enough of
Hammersmith, and Twickenham, and the long journeys into
town. He would take a house wherever he liked, and his friends

would be welcome to stay with him always. To Swift, he promised a home in London for as long as he might like it, 'For you
have been my most generous friend, always.'

'You are a made man, Pope. And you can write whatever you
like,' said Parnell. 'You certainly needn't pretend to be interested
in editing Shakespeare.'

'You are right,' said Pope. 'Thank heaven for that. The very
idea!'

And they all laughed.

Another who was delighted to hear the news was Lord Arden.
He could hardly believe what he heard, and had to ask twice on
what authority it had been published at large. Hearing the details,
he fell to his knees before several others and crossed himself in the
Catholic fashion.

'Friends,' he said at last. 'Forgive this display but I am beside
myself. The years of falsehood are at an end. Never again will I
have to take myself to Church of England services. I can publicly
acknowledge the faith of my fathers, which for years I have had to
keep up entirely privately.' And he started to recite the rosary.

But Mary knew nothing of this. Standing in the garden by the
Queen, waiting in vain for Lady Masham to return, she had no
idea what was happening in the castle – no more than she knew,
as she could then only hope, that she would look back on this
time, thirty years later, as a mother and a grandmother. No more
than she knew that the actions she would herself take, and the
things she would say, in the next few hours would change the
course of history – closing down forever some of the outcomes
most dearly wished for by the people around her, but opening up
other possibilities they had hardly dreamed of.

'Where is Lady Masham?' the Queen asked.

Mary asked if she might perhaps go to look for her, or else fetch some footmen, whichever was quickest.

'You can't leave me, Mary,' the Queen replied. 'Oh, why must she always be absent?'

So they waited again. After ten minutes, the Queen spoke again.

'Mary, I am full of distress . . .'

'Your Majesty! What is it?'

'Mary, I feel sick. My bowels are in a commotion. I have looked in my heart, left no corner untouched, and I cannot feel happy about making my brother my heir. Seeing him, I have felt what guilt was, as if I had never felt it before, but . . .' she stopped, evidently weighing up whether to say something. 'Mary, I some-times see my children. See them now, I mean, as they would have been, had they lived. When I first glimpsed my brother I thought he must be one of them.' And the tears welled up in her eyes.

'When I see them, I talk to them. I ask them what to do. I have talked to them now, and they tell me that if my brother becomes king, as by rights he should have been, instead of me, they would have died in vain. Oh! If I had done the right thing years ago, my father would not have cursed me, and they would still be alive. My beautiful babies.'

Mary was not sure if she should speak or just stay silent, allow-ing the Queen to say what had been closed up inside her for years. But a strong desire to bring comfort impelled her to answer.

'Your Majesty. What is done is done. If you say you did wrong before, and you still have the chance to make it right . . .'

'You think I should? I can't bring them back either way. Oh, Mary, how I wish I knew what I should do. I look in my Bible, and I pray, and I am nothing but a painted hypocrite. The Lord God looks down on me and I feel he is hotly displeased.'

Mary had never been spoken to like this, not by anybody, let alone the Queen of England. She wished that she knew what to do.

The Queen closed her eyes and fell back in her sedan as if in a faint. Mary seized her hand, and felt for a pulse, but that was not necessary because the Queen's massive abdomen continued to rise and fall – she was only sleeping.

Having little alternative, Mary took the great risk of leaving the Queen alone, and in the worst of health, here in the garden, so that she could find people to carry the sedan back inside. She ran as fast as ever she had as a child – something she knew never to do here at court. She soon found a gardener, who stared pitifully at the ground as she spoke to him.

'Please help me. The Queen is in the rose garden. She needs four footmen to carry her back inside. Will you run and find them at once?'

The man nodded, and bowed deeply, before turning and running.

When Mary got back to the Queen, she didn't dare to leave her unexamined. She opened the door of the sedan and patted the Queen's hand, gently at first and then, since that didn't work, with greater force.

'Your Majesty . . . Your Majesty?'

The Queen opened her eyes and at that moment she saw a man walking furtively into the rose garden. He looked about him as if to ensure he was unnoticed, and only too late saw the sedan, with Mary and the Queen inside it.

Defoe fell to his knees.

'Who are you?' the Queen asked.

'My name is Daniel Defoe. We have met before, Your Majesty.'

'Have we?' The Queen was struggling to think straight, to come back to herself.

'I wrote a certain pamphlet, a satire about Dissenters.'

Surprisingly, the Queen remembered it. 'You proposed they should be hanged.'

'I was not in earnest. I am a Dissenter myself.'

'Your satire backfired.'

'But the people understood what I had meant,' Defoe said. 'When I stood in the stocks, they threw only flowers at me.'

'You were fortunate. Men have been hanged for less.'

'Or whipped, or transported,' he agreed. 'I served time at Newgate, Your Majesty. The noise, the roaring and clamour, the stench and nastiness of the afflicted inmates seemed like a vision of hell – and a likely entrance to it.'

'Do you have a wife?'

He nodded.

'Did you not think of your wife?'

'She has always supported my projects, no matter how outlandish, and forgiven the consequences, all too often catastrophic.'

'Have you tried honest work?'

'I have. I have started many trades, kept a good house and clothed my family well. I was never rakish or extravagant. I hoped my children, or grandchildren, would come to be as good gentlemen, statesmen, judges and noblemen as any of higher birth. But French pirates captured my goods and the business was taken from me. We lost everything, and now unless I can find money to repay my debts my maiden sister must be turned out to look for work elsewhere as governess. I myself have already been thrown in

199

prison, not once but three times, by creditors who couldn't agree how to deal with me. I owe my release to the Lord Treasurer.'

'How do you repay him?' the Queen asked.

'I carry out . . . investigations.'

'Is that why you're here?'

Defoe nodded. 'I have made some important discoveries.'

'What do you have to tell us?'

'Part of it concerns a member of your clergy. Dr Jonathan Swift.'

'What about him?'

'Forgive me, but it appears that he is the natural son of Sir William Temple. And his mistress is Sir William's natural daughter. They're brother and sister.'

'Why should that interest Oxford?'

'Swift wants to be a bishop. He hardly seems suitable.'

'Thank you, Dissenter, for taking such care over my church. Have you told Oxford?'

Defoe nodded.

'Have you anything else to report?'

Defoe was desperate. He wanted to tell her something that showed his genius at espionage, something more important than this tittle-tattle about Swift. But he feared to speak directly against the Pretender because the Queen was known to hate speaking of him, and it was possible that she had some affection for the young son of her late father. What could he tell her?

The Queen looked exhausted. But Defoe's silence annoyed her.

'Mr. Defoe, don't make the mistake of confusing physical frailty with an ill-conditioned mind. I'm better informed than people believe. You have continued to write pamphlets?'

'I have.'

'What is the latest one?'

'Oh, Your Majesty, forgive me. It's called "What if the Queen Should Die?"'

'That's a pretty title,' she said, turning to Mary.

Defoe took a copy of the pamphlet from his pocket. 'The full title is "What if the Queen Should Die? What if the Pretender Should Come, or Some Consideration of the Advantages and Real Consequences of the Pretender's Possessing the Crown of Great Britain". It doesn't express my own views. It's a satire.' He put it away again.

'Why do you continue to write what you don't believe? And if you must, why do you suppose everybody else is sincere in what they write?'

'Your Majesty, take care. The Pretender is here at the palace. I have come to tell the Lord Treasurer.'

The Queen whispered to Mary, who walked away towards the castle.

'I beg you, Majesty. You have no more loyal servant.'

'Prove it.'

Defoe could hardly believe what he said next. In his desperation to prove his loyalty, he told her his greatest secret.

'When I was young, I fought for the Duke of Monmouth against your father. The men I fought with were hanged and quartered, and tarred. Even now, to admit I was there is treason. But I tell you because only this can prove how much I hate and fear the tyranny of Rome. Please believe me, the pamphlet is a satire. I have one here, you can read it yourself . . .' He pulled the pamphlet from his pocket. The Queen didn't take it.

Mary returned, and whispered into the Queen's ear.

'I pray you, don't have me arrested.'

'Don't worry. Her errand was less sensational than you imagine. Mary, please remind me: we must send some more money to help Mrs Defoe. Is a hundred pounds enough?'

Defoe couldn't believe it.

'Oh your Majesty, God bless you! But the Lord Treasurer has pledged me five thousand pounds already.'

The Queen looked amazed. 'Five thousand?'

A group of footmen arrived. One of them carried a chamber pot — the same footman, with fine blond hair, who saw Defoe kill Nottingham's man the previous evening. He handed the pot to Mary, who handed it to the Queen, and closed the door of the sedan. The footman stepped towards Mary and whispered.

'My lady, that man's dangerous. He killed the Earl of Nottingham's man. I saw it. It was an accident, but if he recognises me he may be desperate.'

Mary thanked him, but gave no sign of alarm. When the Queen had finished, Mary gave him back the chamber pot and he left at once. Then the others lifted the sedan and started to carry it towards the castle. Mary beckoned Defoe toward her.

In an instant, she decided to use this man to help her. He looked desperate, but essentially honest, and her instinct told her what to do.

'I know who you are,' she whispered. 'You killed the Earl of Nottingham's man. Don't speak, just listen. I need your help. If you don't do exactly as I instruct, you'll hang.'

The Church of Rome promised eternal damnation for apostates like Lord Arden

Chapter 25

The Lord Woundeth, and His Hands Make Whole

Defoe felt desperate. Nothing had gone right. He'd failed to secure even one scrap of evidence about Swift and Oxford would never pay him after the disaster of the previous night. He had failed to eliminate the Pretender, and now he had confessed to treason against the Pretender's father before a lady-in-waiting who he felt sure was the daughter of Lord Arden – a Catholic, albeit a lapsed one. And, worse than that, she knew he had killed a man.

Defoe was a tough character who had witnessed enough hangings to watch unmoved as the criminal danced at the end of his rope. But knowing that this was to be his own fate changed everything. He would never again see his lovely wife and children, and could do nothing to protect them and support them. He felt his heart sink in despair, and tears rolled down his cheeks. He looked about him at the open space of the garden but knew he could never run away. For so long he had been full of pride, believing himself able to go anywhere, and learn anything, without being caught, and now the Lord had cast him down, a wicked creature in the dunghill. But just as he approached despair, he remembered that even in the teeth of the lion in the wilderness, grace and mercy were possible. The Lord woundeth, and His hands make whole. Only God could save him.

Defoe wiped away the tears as they neared the French doors that would take them back inside the castle. He decided he would help this young woman as much as he possibly could. After all, she had said he would hang only if he did not do exactly as she instructed.

And so it was that, in the hour and more that the Queen slumbered, and Lady Masham was nowhere to be found, and the Queen's ministers prepared to meet again in her cabinet, Defoe told Mary everything about how Nottingham's man had died, and why Defoe was in the castle, and how he glimpsed the Pretender in Lady Masham's room, and what he had seen in Arbuthnot's rooms, even including what Bolingbroke said to Oxford about lost German lives. And he told her how he had smashed his pistol into the Pretender's face and broken into the lodgings Swift shared with Pope, and what he learned there, but he sensed that this hardened the girl's heart against him, so he told her about his beloved wife and beautiful children, in the hope that this might soften her heart again.

And it worked! Because then the girl told him some secrets of her own, about her love for a certain Whig (which he knew already), and her desire that her father might be brought around to permitting her to marry him — but only if a certain event could be brought to pass — and then she told Defoe something quite sensational about Lady Masham not only smuggling the Pretender into the castle but also stealing money from the Queen. After they had shared this information they looked at each other with fresh eyes, the older man and the young woman with such very different lives.

And before waking the Queen, Mary sent messages containing certain information to Samuel, and to her father, conjuring them to meet each other at once and be friends, and come as soon as they could to the Queen's cabinet.

The Duchess had endured more than Lady Masham gave her credit for

Chapter 26

A Last Chance to Amend
the Succession

Oxford was going in to see the Queen. At the door, he met Dr Arbuthnot. The doctor shook his head grimly, as if to say that the Queen had only a few hours left to live.

Bolingbroke arrived. Together, the two estranged ministers went in. Then another man arrived, the leader of the opposition, Robert Walpole, and the magical effect of his appearance was to make Oxford and Bolingbroke appear like friends again.

Without waiting for permission to speak, Walpole addressed the Queen directly.

'Your Majesty, the Elector of Hanover has been informed about your recent ill health. He has ventured to begin his journey from Germany, and looks forward to finding you here.'

The Queen put on her spectacles and glowered at him.

'Is the throne empty? Must he steal what will be his, in a few hours, without offence?'

Bolingbroke got down on his knees. 'Your Majesty, I beg you. This is your last chance to amend the succession against him.'

At that moment, the Queen started to vomit. When she had

finished, a long silence followed, in which everybody present looked from one to another, then cast their eyes upon the floor.

Eventually, she replied: 'I will do what I must. Mr Walpole, you can come back in half an hour.'

'Your Majesty.' Walpole bowed to her, then to the ministers, who did not bow back.

'Do get up,' she said to Bolingbroke. 'I can't do what you ask. It would mean nothing. The Act of Settlement was designed to keep Catholics off the throne. My father's son has never offered to change his faith.'

Bolingbroke got up and moved along the bed towards her. She had never previously referred to the Pretender as her father's son. This seemed promising. 'Laws can be changed. And once he has taken possession of what rightly belongs to him, only bloody revolution would remove him.'

'Don't you think we have had enough bloody revolution?' she replied. And she vomited again.

Oxford took a letter from his pocket.

'Your Majesty, I have a letter from your brother. He forgives you from the bottom of his heart.'

'I suspected that Bolingbroke corresponded with the crown's enemies. Not you. Where's Lady Masham?'

Oxford went to the door and whispered to a footman, then came back.

'She has not been seen for hours, Your Majesty,' he said.

The Queen slumped back in her bed. After a long pause, Bolingbroke leaned over her and addressed Dr Arbuthnot.

'See that feather on her pillow? It's not moving. This sleep is sound indeed.'

'Are we too late?'

They looked at Mary, wondering what they could safely discuss before her – even at this late stage, people continued to overlook her. But after a moment, the Queen stirred again.

'Open the window,' she said at last. 'The heat is killing me.'

Rather than wait for a servant, Oxford did as she asked himself.

Bolingbroke spoke next.

'Madam, your father, who loved you, lies unburied in Paris, in a coffin at the church of the English Benedictines. His remains wait only to be brought home after your brother regains the throne.'

'How could I do for the boy what I never could do for my father?' the Queen asked. 'Why did nobody plead for him? Who, in my youthful folly, kneeled at my feet and told me that he loved me, till it was too late?'

'It's not too late for your brother,' said Oxford.

At that moment, the doors opened and a footman announced Lord Arden and Samuel Holland. The ministers looked surprised.

'What do they want?' asked Bolingbroke.

The two men walked in, and both bowed extremely low to the Queen, then at the ministers. Mary noticed that they avoided looking directly at Bolingbroke or Oxford.

'Your Majesty,' said Mary's father. 'We have a matter of the utmost gravity to tell you, and beg leave to deliver the message privately.'

'That's impossible,' said Bolingbroke. 'We are the Queen's chief ministers.'

'I will decide that, my lord,' said the Queen. 'Lord Arden, Mr

Holland, please step towards my bed. You others can move off a little. Thank you.'

The two men walked together to the Queen's bedside. They had evidently not yet agreed who should speak, but Samuel graciously gave way. And while Mary's father delivered the message Samuel looked around the room for a sight of her. They exchanged glances, but both knew better than to smile, considering the gravity of the moment.

Having heard what Lord Arden had to say, the Queen glanced first at Bolingbroke, then at Oxford. In a low voice, she asked a question, perhaps seeking some kind of clarification, and Samuel leaned over to answer her.

'Thank you,' she said, and the two withdrew to the back of the room.

Then she turned to her ministers.

'My lords, please can you tell me how you intend to make up for the German lives you have sacrificed?'

They looked appalled. Bolingbroke was first to speak:

'When I was in Paris,' he said, 'concluding peace on your behalf, Oxford leaked our battle plans to the French generals. Many of our German allies lost their lives as a result. If George of Hanover becomes king, and discovers what we did, we will hang.'

'We acted in your own interests,' said Oxford. 'We put an end to the bloody war, saving the lives of countless Englishmen.'

'But thousands died to protect our Protestant faith,' said the Queen. 'I'm not going to acknowledge a Catholic merely to save your careers. Do you not care that God watches you?'

'I grant that Bolingbroke cares little for the church. But don't accuse me of that.'

'Then why do you plead for the promotion of a godless clergy-man?' the Queen asked. 'Jonathan Swift is an adulterer, and his mistress is his sister. You ask me to make him a bishop. As history shall judge, the one thing that justifies my reign is my support of the Church of England.'

'Swift has served you faithfully as a clergyman and a pamphlet-eer,' said Oxford. 'I count the man a friend and know nothing of his private life.'

'You took five thousand pounds from my private purse to pay Daniel Defoe for evidence about Swift's incest. Mary, bring out Defoe.'

The effort of holding her own against the ministers was visibly weakening the Queen. She was short of breath, and her face had turned red.

Mary fetched Defoe from behind a tapestry. As he came out, and looked at Oxford, Defoe felt a terrible emptiness. This man had been a second father to him. Only a short time earlier, he believed that Oxford cared more for him even than his wife.

'Traitor!' said Oxford, and the word felt like a knife in Defoe's heart. What had he done? 'I did it to protect Swift's reputation. He's a friend. Was that wrong?'

'Forget Swift,' said the Queen. 'There are more important things. If I died without removing you, you would call in the Pretender against my wishes. Give me the white staff.'

Oxford handed her the symbol of his office.

'It's not us who should think of God,' shouted Bolingbroke, desperate now. 'It's you. You betrayed your father, King James, and God punished you for it. Before you go to meet your maker, pray for forgiveness and make right what you did wrong.'

'If I did what you wish, then falling out with my father in the first place would have been for nothing. My children would still be alive if he had not cursed me. If I change my mind now, it will not bring them back. Only one person has shown me kindness in daring to reconcile me to my brother – dear Abigail.'

Mary was desperate to speak out against Lady Masham, but she couldn't bring herself to smash the Queen's illusions. Defoe, seeing that she said nothing, wondered if he might say something himself, without it being obvious that Mary had told him. He was not sure it would work, but he had no time before the Queen said: 'Mary, fetch back Mr Walpole. Summon the privy council. They must help to choose Oxford's successor. And please find dear Abigail.'

Mary left the room. Defoe seized his chance. 'Your Majesty, I beg to speak before the privy council arrives. It seems the Lord Treasurer is not the honest man I took him for, but there is another who has betrayed your trust.'

'Who?' the Queen asked.

'Lady Masham. She has been stealing your money.'

'I don't believe it.' She vomited again. And again, a terrible long silence followed. Was this the end?

Not yet. After the sickness passed, Defoe spoke.

'Madam, I overheard Lady Masham speaking of it with Bolingbroke last night. I came to the castle to spy for the Lord Treasurer. Ask Lady Masham to reveal the contents of a secret pocket under her skirts. There is money, and papers, she stole from you.'

'Impossible.'

Bolingbroke interrupted. 'It's true. Lady Masham did steal your money. But you will not find her because she's with the

Pretender, probably hurrying into fresh exile as we speak. And now, if you'll excuse me, I must join them.'

He walked out. Oxford too moved towards the door. Defoe rushed to block his way.

'Don't leave,' Defoe said. 'Think of your family.'

Oxford stopped, but looked furious. 'You prig. All this, just to discredit Swift? What harm has he done you? I don't suppose he even knows you exist. Where is your evidence against him?'

Defoe was heartbroken to discover the truth about the man he had admired above all others. He felt as if he were split in half. But in this moment his outrage was stronger than his pity. 'You know my suspicions are true. You only want evidence to destroy it.'

The privy council arrived and crowded around the Queen's bed.

Oxford stayed for a moment, but Defoe watched him move to the back and leave shortly before the Queen said: 'My lords, you have waited for me to do something decisive. I may have left it too late.' She was breathing extremely faintly now. 'My ministers desert me, and my power is going. Is Lord Arden still here?'

He stepped forward.

'My lord, I have no time to tell you all you need to know – that your daughter is a lovely young woman, with a good heart. That, of course, you know already. I would give anything for a daughter so lovely of my own. But you should know too that she loves Samuel Holland. I advise you to let them marry. George of Hanover is coming, and you would do well to choose a prominent Whig for your son-in-law.' She paused. 'Now, lords, the country needs a prime minister. I beg you to choose him for me. And remember me to my successors.'

213

Chapter 27

A Woman of Little Importance

That was not quite the last thing the Queen did, mind you. While the privy council were with her she let it be known that she wished the Pretender be allowed to escape from the castle, and from England, without any further injury.

'You may recognise him,' she said, 'if you see him, by the dark bruises around his eyes.'

And that's what happened. The word got out, and when Lady Masham emerged from her rooms, finally carrying the paper and ink she had promised the Queen hours before, she was quick to hear the terrible news. She hurried back, only to find the captain of the Queen's guard outside her door, a great hound straining at the leash in his hand.

She stopped, aghast, and started to protest, but the man explained the Queen's wish, and added, as gently as he could, that the Queen wished never again to lay eyes on Her Ladyship.

And in a short time afterward the Pretender was back at court in Paris, rejoicing in the title of James III of England, a title that the French nobility, if nobody else, were willing to grant him, and plotting the attack on England that he would launch, without success, the following year. He never gave up his claim to the throne.

Lady Masham returned home with her husband, trying hard not to despise him and to behave towards her various offspring as if they really did have the same father.

Viscount Bolingbroke made it to France, only to return many years later — but he would never achieve anything like his former eminence again. The Earl of Oxford stayed in England, his treason against England's German allies remained secret during his lifetime, and he died peacefully.

Walpole was selected by the privy council as the country's prime minister — the first to take that title — and confirmed in the role by the new King, George I. One of Walpole's first appointments to the new King's government was Samuel Holland, in a junior position but on the understanding that higher office would follow if he did as he was told and took care at all times to crush Tories under his feet like serpents and creeping things.

Samuel was unwilling to stay in office for long on these terms, not least because he grew to feel a greater respect than ever for his Tory father-in-law. He quit politics and went to live in Herefordshire, where he gained a reputation as a fair and generous landlord, capable of embracing technological developments without at the same time destroying the livelihoods, and the hopes, of those people who had worked for him using more time-honoured methods. He raised his children in the Church of England but never had a bad word for the Church of Rome.

As Samuel's wife, Mary lived a full life that, though it was punctuated with difficulties like any other, she looked back on, in her old age, entirely with satisfaction. Nobody who met her could ever have imagined that somebody so modest, and gentle, could possibly have directed the course of history, and decided the fate of kings — but Mary knew the truth.

And Defoe? One summer, late in the reign of George I, Defoe walked into the kitchen, carrying a basket of gooseberries, and showed it to Sarah.

She put down her sewing — a cap for their latest grandchild — and took the basket.

Defoe took off his dusty boots, felt the cold stone floor beneath his feet, and turned to look back at the garden. The sun was low in the sky, and the full moon had risen. It hung high above the nearby woods.

He sighed deeply.

'What are you thinking?' Sarah asked.

Still his first instinct told him to be secretive, to deny that he was even thinking at all. But he had learned by now to share the truth.

'I was consumed, for an instant, by pride. You have saved me.'

That night, as they lay in darkness, drifting towards a peaceful night's sleep, Sarah asked: 'Pride in what?'

He laughed.

'My gooseberry harvest. My house. My wife. My children and grandchildren. And, if I'm really honest, my *Robinson Crusoe*. It has sold better than ever I hoped — and I finished it long before Swift published *Gulliver*.'

'God has blessed you.'

'I know it. And I feel it. When I feel it, I'm grateful. And when I'm grateful, my profit and loss account weighs heavily in my favour.'

'You're a good man, Daniel Defoe.'

'Thank you. But not as good as I once thought I was. In my pride, I tried to do God's own work. To decide the fate of kings. And it turned me into a lunatic.'

'You helped to see off the threat of Catholic tyranny.'
'And in doing so, I destroyed my patron.'
'Not everything turned out as you wanted it.'
And it was so good to be surprised.

What comes next?

Finished. Made it. It's done.

Did it go as planned?

Not quite.

Is there nothing left to wish for?

Of course there is. But it can always be useful to look back – to work out how we got from there to here.

IT'S ALL ME, ME, ME

I was always looking for stories. Things to write about in the papers, or for glossy magazines. Alongside the more conventional forays into print, I had tried many trades. I especially liked things that I could immerse myself in, like the great American journalists of the 1970s. Like the time I worked as an undertaker's assistant. Or when I launched myself off the side of the tallest building in London to clean its windows. Or when I got in the ring with a professional boxer.

My friend and former colleague Richard Cook used to tease me: *It's all about you, isn't it, Japes? It's all me, me, me* . . . But putting myself in the story felt more honest than the spurious objectivity that other journalists sometimes hid behind. That's what I told him, anyway. I'm in there as a representative of the reader, I said. The things that happened to me might have happened to them. My struggles are their struggles.

He looked sceptical.

WOW! BRILLIANT! AMAZING!

And he was probably right – because I did also just like having adventures. One time, I persuaded a magazine editor to let me join the cast of a London pantomime, from the start of rehearsals and into performance, and write it up for the special Christmas issue.

I was looking for another experience like that when I bought a second-hand copy of Keith Johnstone's book, *Impro: Improvisation and the Theatre*. It had many pencil marks, including ecstatic comments, in the margins. From the start, I was gripped by the book's account of the extraordinary work Johnstone had done, first with school children and then at The Royal Court theatre in its 1950s heyday. He devised games to teach people to be more spontaneous, collaborative and creative. I thought, *I want some of that*. By the time I had finished reading it, then finished reading it again several times, the margins contained considerably more ecstatic comments. ('Ha!' 'Wow!' 'Brilliant!' 'Amazing!' and 'This book is so good!')

If only Johnstone had been alive. I'd have leapt at the chance to see him at work, and interview him – perhaps for the *Sunday Times*. A story about this legendary theatre man would be fun to write – and would bring in much needed funds.

KEITH IS ALIVE!

But what made me think he was dead? He wasn't. He had just moved to Canada.

BE MY GUINEA PIG

And a bit of exploring on the Internet led to the discovery that he still taught, occasionally. So I signed up for the first of several weeks' training with him, and on a warm day in September I found myself in a large room with thirty or so actors from all over the world – whom I didn't know – and Keith (as everybody called him) sitting opposite them on a big sofa.

A few months before, I received a call from a friend – a woman I admire and respect. Fenella said, 'I'm training as a coach', and she asked me if I would be one of her clients.

To be honest, I had no idea what coaching meant. My gut reaction was that it sounded a bit silly. I agreed to do it – but only as a favour to Fenella.

CONVERSATIONS THAT CHANGE EVERYTHING

I soon found myself amazed by the effect of a conversation that was both supportive and challenging.

PROSPECTS AS A WRITER

One of the things that came up a lot on those conversations was the question of my prospects as a writer.

As a child I'd always loved reading, and dreamed of writing. At school I'd experimented by borrowing from the great writers of the past. At university, studying English literature, I had especially loved Shakespeare, Jane Austen, James Joyce, Mary Shelley, Lord Byron, and I'd written half of my Master's thesis in rhyming couplets, in homage to Alexander Pope. I left university hoping to become a poet myself – and only realised slowly that I was unlikely to make a living that way.

So I became a journalist instead. And after a few years, I had one of the best jobs there is: a magazine writer on a national newspaper.

WHO'S A WRITER YOU ADMIRE?

Fenella said, 'Who is a writer you particularly admire?'

I went blank. Where to start? As she knew already, I liked lots of great writers.

After a very long pause, I thought of a name. 'Gyles Brandreth.'

She didn't manage entirely to conceal her surprise.

'OK,' she said. 'What do you particularly like about Gyles Brandreth?'

'A lot of things.'

'Such as?'

I had interviewed him for the *Financial Times* when he published a book about Queen Elizabeth II's consort, Prince Philip. I had come away feeling nothing but admiration – for his evident intelligence, his sense of humour, his versatility. He'd been a senior figure in Parliament, he'd interviewed all kinds of interesting people for the papers, written books, presented TV and radio shows, and performed his own one-man show. He was prolific, and well known. He seemed to be pleased with himself, and not unduly worried that some people might think him too pleased with himself.

'It sounds like you have described the person you would like to be,' Fenella said.

A NOVEL IDEA

Another time, Fenella asked me: 'Have you ever thought of writing a novel?'

And I said, 'I practically finished a novel once. But that was long ago.'

WHAT WOULD SHAKESPEARE WRITE?

I'd always liked Shakespeare. I studied Shakespeare and his influence for my Master's. And after my first book came out, in the late 1990s, I met an old school friend and the topic of Shakespeare came up.

Sebastian had become a screenwriter. We chatted about stories and we started to wonder – which king or queen would Shakespeare have written about if he had lived to hear about them?

We ran through the list, and quickly decided it would be James II. His father, Charles I, was beheaded by Cromwell. He lived in exile as a young man until his older brother, Charles II, was restored to the throne. Then, on inheriting the throne himself, he made the stupid mistake of announcing that he was a Catholic – in a country that hated Catholics. One of his nephews raised a rebellion against him, which he defeated, but soon after he got scared and ran off to France with his young second wife and their baby son. In his absence, the country was ruled by his grown-up daughters, who had been brought up Protestant.

But then we thought it might be more interesting to look at one of those daughters, Queen Anne.

'OK,' said Fenella. 'But don't tell me her story. Tell me what happened to the book.'

REJECTION

Well, I wrote a lot of it – about half – in spare weekends, on sabbatical and in holidays, when I worked at the *Financial Times*.

I gave it to my agent, a very high-powered agent, who sent it to a few publishers. I hoped that they might give me a decent advance – actually pay me to write the rest. After all, I'd become used to being paid for my writing. It was how I paid the mortgage. I only want what any man might ask for – a secure living.

The rejection letters, when they eventually arrived, felt painful. Not terribly painful, but painful enough. I put the book aside. I threw myself back into journalism. My agent moved abroad.

STEPPING INTO MY COFFIN

But people stopped buying newspapers, and the *Financial Times* needed to cut jobs. The editor decided that he no longer needed a magazine writer on staff, with a pension scheme and holidays and so on. Instead, I was offered a different job – a boring job, a job I would have hated. It felt like I was being invited to step into my coffin. So I took voluntary redundancy. I could have been plunged into despair by the loss of my patron, but instead I got myself a contract to write the same kinds of stories, as a freelancer, for the *Sunday Times*.

'Did you ever finish the novel?'

No. I pretended, for as long as I could, that the routine work still interested me, and would continue to provide a secure income. But it didn't, and it wouldn't. The *Sunday Times* started cutting back too . . . What could I do to secure myself?

'You keep talking about these other things – are you avoiding talking about the book?'

'Maybe.'

'Would you like to finish it?'

'Yes.' The answer surprised me.

'Will you?'

'Yes.'

Again I was surprised – but also excited to hear myself say

it. Fenella's questions gave me permission to do something I wanted to do but had somehow forgotten.

'When will you start?'

'Monday.'

'When will you finish?'

'October.'

WHAT COMES NEXT?

Keith taught us a game, What Comes Next? You play it in pairs, making up a story one sentence at a time.

If you're the listener, and if you like a sentence from your partner, you just say, 'Yes! What comes next?' And they continue to make things up, one sentence at a time. But if for any reason you don't like the way the story is going, you say, 'No', and take over the storytelling yourself.

If both players are honest, and say no to the things they don't want, the story will necessarily be one you both enjoyed.

The first time I played it was with an actor from Denmark, Pernille Sorensen. I don't remember the whole story, but I remember we flew an imaginary plane together, both holding imaginary steering wheels as we whizzed around the room, then up into the clouds, where we met God.

Weirdly, I felt slightly blessed afterwards. And I remembered something that one of the other performers had told me. Ouardane Jouannot, from France, was not an actor by trade but a scientist. He told me he did improvisation because he wanted to experience things he would otherwise never experience.

What did he mean?

'Well, I always wondered what it must be like to be a person who wants a sex change. I don't want a sex change, and I have never understood that. But by playing a scene with other people, I came to understand it. Now I know, at least a bit. If you perform it, it becomes real. The same parts of your brain are involved as if it was really happening.'

At the time, I was not sure I believed Ouardane, but after playing lots of games, and improvising several scenes, I was convinced.

But enjoying the story doesn't mean it has to be nice. Sometimes you want to say, 'Ooh! yes, what comes next?' to things you would never wish to happen in real life.

I CUT YOUR BOLLOCKS OFF

Another time, I played with Steve Chapman. We had a fight, and we enacted it as it unfolded – Keith particularly encouraged us to enact it. At one point Steve's sentence was, *I cut your bollocks off*. 'Yes,' I said, 'what comes next?' 'You scream,' he said. 'No.' He said: 'What comes next?' I said, 'I poke your eye out.' 'Yes,' he said, 'what comes next?' 'The eyeball falls down a drain.' 'Yes, what comes next?' 'I poke the other eyeball out.' 'No. What comes next?' 'I try to open the drain, and you run away.' 'Yes, what comes next?' 'I run after you.' 'Yes, what comes next?' 'We find ourselves on railway tracks and hear the train coming.' 'Yes, what comes next?' 'We run away from the train?' 'Yes, what comes next?' 'We escape.' 'No. What comes next?' 'We turn around to see the train just as it's about to hit us.' 'Yes, what comes next?' 'We scream, and – the End.'

'Yes.'

Another time, I played a competitive game of What Comes Next? with my friend Robert Twigger, the adventurer and author. We both supplied sentences to a third person, Janine, who chose between what we offered her. If she liked the way Twigger took our story, we both continued with that. Or, if Janine preferred mine, we went with that. (If she didn't like either suggestion, we had to come up with more.)

Over time, it became clear what kind of storylines Janine wanted – something mystical, or magical like a fairytale appealed much more than violence or crude humour. But every audience is different. To make it competitive, Keith appointed somebody to count the number of times Janine chose my line or Twigger's. With an audience watching us, it felt like high stakes. I won, but only by a couple of points.

MAKE BETTER OFFERS

Playing What Comes Next? taught us the value of an honest response to what we are being offered, and made us better at offering things people might like. But training with Keith, which I continued to do for years afterwards, taught me to see that I will never stop failing. I will never Get It All Right, or please everybody, and it will always hurt, but perhaps not quite so much.

Once, Keith asked us to improvise anything, solo, in front of the rest of the group – and he instructed members of the audience to leave their seats and walk out quietly as soon as they lost interest in what we were doing. When half the audience had gone, we had to stop.

Several people lost half the audience after less than five seconds. I managed to keep going for fifteen seconds.

'What's important about this?' asked Fenella.

'Well, it was painful to see them leave, but it provided a useful lesson, when they explained why they lost interest.'

'Anything else? We've got five more minutes . . .'

'Yes. More important than that – it was such fun to work together. Not just in that game, but generally. The creativity that came out of improvisation, working together without any preparation. It felt a lot more enjoyable than doing lots of heavy research, alone at my desk, then typing it all up, alone at my desk.'

'What are you thinking?'

'Well, it might be fun if I asked the improvisers to help me finish my Queen Anne book.'

'Will you do that?'

Her question surprised me. Why would they want to help?

'Why wouldn't they? What are you offering them?'

'I don't know. A chance to play? And I could bring some food.'

'If you ask them, do they have to say yes?'

'No. OK, I'll ask them.'

'Great. Now our time's up.'

WOULD ANYBODY COME?

I recorded a video message to all the improvisers I knew, telling them I had almost finished the novel but was keen to explore some of the scenes with them.

I said, 'It's about Queen Anne, but don't worry because nobody seems to know anything about Queen Anne, and anyway, it's better not to do any research.' I put the video on YouTube.

I booked a room in a community centre, and on the night before, I baked two loaves of bread and filled a box with cheese, salad, and jam.

Would anybody come?

I PLAYED THE QUEEN

The first person to arrive at the community centre was my dear friend Twigger, bless him. Then came an actor, Roses Urquhart. Then Pernille, who had come to London from Denmark. Later, we were joined by Olly Hawes, and Barbara le Lan, and David Kershaw.

I told them that I'd largely finished writing the book but wanted to explore the back story, to work out why Anne, and the people around her, might have behaved the way they did. Later, if we had time, I wanted to try some of the scenes in the book, to see if they could be more interesting another way.

For several hours, we performed scenes from Anne's youth. Her response to her father's second marriage. How George of Hanover visited England to propose marriage to her, but humiliated her by deciding not to. How she managed to be absent from the birth of her Catholic half-brother (and how this distressed her father). And how she felt when her father, from exile in France, cursed her for taking his throne.

We played some scenes several times, and took turns playing

different characters or observing. At one point, I wanted to know what exactly triggered James to curse his daughter, so we tried it. Roses played James and I played his young Italian wife. Robert played the little Pretender, sitting under a table, comfort-eating as his parents blew up around him, in exile in France. King James got into a towering rage, shouting as he broke a pen writing his curse on Anne and all her children. The young queen got down on her knees, begging him to be once again the man she had married. As the queen, I was surprised but pleased that this plea did subdue the exiled king a little.

Pernille made a suggestion. She said she might ask us to pause, at times, and would ask one of us to speak aloud the inner thoughts of our character. Or perhaps she would ask all of us to do this at once, so that she could wander round and listen to us individually.

When this happened, it felt like I was watching something miraculous. How did these people who knew so little about the characters in my book contrive to invent, spontaneously, such rich and plausible material? It was as if they instinctively knew everyone's stories already.

A part of me wished that I had been able to capture every word – but I sensed that the process might have been compromised by the knowledge that what we were doing was being recorded. People behave differently when they are conscious of being watched.

So most of it was lost. But a powerful sense of the scenes remains with me still – and of the magic that can happen when I ask people to help.

WHAT COMES NEXT?

Oh, don't be daft. Everybody knows what comes next: Queen Anne dies, and she's succeeded by George I. It takes two seconds on Google to find that out, so the outcome is known already. There's no uncertainty. It's actually very boring.

So make it less boring. Do something unexpected. What comes next?

Anne decides, as she's dying, to favour the Pretender.

Yes, what comes next?

All the Catholics reveal themselves to have been hoping for this all along. They recite the rosary, that kind of thing.

Yes. Do it.

TRANSPORTED A LITTLE

Sometime later, I asked my friend Ben Spencer to contact the improvisers and to interview them on camera. Here's some of what Ben's interviewees told him.

Twigger: When you're writing, you write a piece, and rewrite it and rewrite it. John-Paul had done a lot of that, and I didn't think he wanted to do more of it. But improvising, with different people playing all the different roles, you could do it all in one go. So I was into it, and we spent a day doing it. It was one of the most interesting experiences I've ever had.

Olly: John-Paul had baked some sourdough bread, and there

was a selection of deli treats to go with it. He said: 'Oh, hello, Olly. Come in.' And we proceeded to play for a number of hours.

Pernille: When you work this way, you're in a sort of trance, a flow, where you're both conscious and unconscious of what's going on. What I sensed was that this woman, Queen Anne, had been through many tragic things in her life that made her very strong and very vulnerable at the same time. And of course, even though she was a queen, she had the same emotions, the same love, as every mother would have for her children.

Olly: I can remember vividly a particular moment. We ran improvisations about what would happen. We ran it three times. The first time there was a lot of love, relief and joy. The second time, there was anger, and harsh words spoken. And the third time, when I was playing Queen Anne, she said nothing. She refused to engage. It proved to be this really electrifying, interesting thing that can happen sometimes when you are acting something out. One moment you are sat in a fluorescent-lit community centre off the Edgware Road, and the next moment you are transported a little bit. It provoked some interesting, intriguing discussions and responses.

Pernille: John-Paul has a playful approach to what he does when he creates material. That's the way new art forms, new things, really interesting things come up – when you have a curiosity, and a playfulness, and a generosity in your way of working.

After the others had gone home, I left the building with Twigger. We congratulated ourselves on having (so we thought)
invented a whole new way for authors to collaborate. We
looked forward to doing it with other authors in future. I
turned my phone on and picked up a message from a brilliant
improviser, Jude Claybourne. She said she had been wandering
around Edgware Road for hours, looking for the community
centre, but hadn't been able to find us. I felt bad, but still also
elated.

WHAT COMES NEXT?

Swift says: Our hero wakes up, only to find that he's been tied
down – by his hair.

Pope: Yes! What comes next?

Swift: The person who tied him down is an embittered, vindic-
tive thief.

Pope: No.

Swift: What comes next?

Pope: He's been tied down by hundreds of tiny people, and
they're crawling all over him.

Swift: Yes. What comes next?

YOUR FACE HERE?

Over the following days, I hastily wrote up as much as I could remember of that extraordinary day of improvisation.

I wanted to do more, somehow, to bring the characters alive in my head – and also to acknowledge the contribution of others. I came up with an idea for illustrations – superimposing on to contemporary portraits of my characters the faces of my improviser friends.

I sent a message to a group of them. The first to reply was Will Steele. I asked if he would be Parnell. He immediately said yes. So I sent instructions that were highly specific and probably also unreasonable: *Could you take a picture of yourself*, I asked, *with the camera looking down at you slightly? Your expression is bursting with pride but you're trying to hide it and are slightly afraid that you might lose everything any minute.*

I asked Hermione Jones to be Lady Mary. By way of background, I said only that she sees and hears more than the plotters around her suspect. *Can you hint at that knowledge with a sparkle in your eye?*

I asked Pernille to be Lady Masham. Tony Quinn to be Bolingbroke. Ouardane Jouannot to be the Pretender and Daniel Dresner, my new coach, to be Defoe. Their pictures made me very happy.

And Anne? I asked Jude, the improviser who got lost.

I distorted the modern portraits, posterised them, turned them black and white, framed them, placed them over the contemporary portraits, inserted them into the manuscript and sent it off to publishers. Surely, I thought, they'll be falling over themselves to publish this.

MARKETING WILL BE DIFFICULT

Over coffee, one publisher said she thought the book was great, but marketing it would be difficult. I told her about the unusual process by which I had picked up writing it again – the coaching I'd had. The improvisation in the community centre. She looked a lot more interested now, perhaps even persuaded that there were some good opportunities for marketing – but she had said no already, and I didn't want to ask her again.

THE DEFINITION OF SUCCESS

Over another coffee, on another day, in another fashionable coffee house, I talked it over with Steve, the improviser who had cut off my bollocks before I poked his eyes out.

Steve had written a book of his own, a book about spontaneity and creativity, illustrated by his daughter, Maya, and he had published it himself. I had given him encouragement, a few practical tips, and at his request I had filmed his improvised 'Busking Book Launch' on London's South Bank. Using a few chords on his guitar, he made up songs about the book to attract the attention of passersby. He had shifted many copies before finally we were moved on, for busking without a licence.

I admired Steve's single-mindedness. He seemed to know

what he needed to do, and he did it, even if it meant pushing himself into situations that others might find awkward, potentially even shameful. As a result, he'd achieved what he set out to do: the only true measure of success.

But what would be my definition of success? In all the years I'd been writing this novel, the one you are now reading, I had never stopped to give the question much thought. At best, I had probably done no more than wish, vaguely, that it would be published by a prestigious publisher, it would get good reviews, and people would be impressed.

But what does that mean exactly? What makes a publisher prestigious? And what makes a review 'good'? Does it need to be prominent? How prominent? Does it need to have a photograph of me on the page somewhere? Does it need to say Very Clever Things that I didn't even know myself about the book? And how many people needed to be impressed? One? Fourteen? Half a million? And did it matter if just as many people – or more – were not impressed at all? Or were, in fact, distinctly unimpressed?

I tried hard to work out what exactly a successful outcome might look like. But it kept escaping me, because there was always more detail to be considered. A part of me seemed to believe it was possible to imagine in advance how it would all finally work out – the bits of plot I hadn't quite tied up, and everything about the finished artefact: the cover, the typesetting. But it was impossible. Like the characters in my novel, I could never know how things were going to work out until it was all over.

So I tried to become a kind of connoisseur of uncertainty – enjoying the not-knowing rather than hating it. After all, that was one of the things that drew me to improvisation, where the lack of a script is a wonderful guarantee of freedom.

I said much of this to Steve. And he said: 'It sounds like you want to combine the novel with an account of how you created it.'

I hadn't thought of it like that. But I liked the idea. And it suddenly dawned on me that a whole new opportunity had become real, yet again, only because I'd talked it over with someone willing to listen.

WHAT COMES NEXT?

Defoe poisons the Queen.

No.

What comes next? Defoe tries to poison the Pretender.

Yes! What comes next?

Lady Masham takes the poisoned drink to the Queen.

Yes! What comes next?

The Queen dies, but it's not absolutely clear that Defoe caused it.

Yes. That will do.

BEAUTIFUL OBJECTS

At Wigtown Book Festival, I met one of Twigger's friends. Tahir Shah had come to talk about a book he had published himself. He had a long list of books he'd published with 'proper' publishers, but clearly relished the experience of writing, designing and printing his book *Scorpion Soup*. It was a beautiful object, with many beautiful maps inside it. Tahir talked cheerfully about how useless many publishers could be, and made the point that many authors have to do their own marketing anyway. I became aware that some publishers who heard him found Tahir annoying – to say the least – but to me it was exciting to see somebody with such cheerful self-belief. We became friends.

Because of Steve, and Tahir, I started to think seriously about self-publishing my Queen Anne novel. It wouldn't be such a big step, because for a long time now I've been printing off my work-in-progress in book form.

Even when I'm nowhere near finished, I hate to read what I've written on loose sheets of paper. If it's going to be a book, I want to read it as a book. Sometimes I hand-bind it. Or else I upload it to a company called Lulu.com, and print off single copies, typeset and designed by me. This book you are holding in your hands had already been printed six times in book form, with six different covers, by the time I found myself typing this sentence.

But if I was to sell those copies, I would need to get higher resolution on the covers that I designed, typically, on my phone. So I called a couple of designer friends. I outlined Queen Anne's story, and how I'd gone about writing it.

BE MORE AMBITIOUS

'Sounds great,' said Tina.

'But you know what? I think you could be a bit more ambitious,' said Mike. 'If you do it all yourself, and print a few copies to sell on your website, how will anybody know about it? How many people come to your website to buy anything?'

None. But what else could I do?

'Why don't you crowd-fund it?'

I knew what the words meant, but not really what it involved.

'It's like a marketing campaign, to build up interest in your book before it's published. You raise the money first, so you know you won't make a loss – you make a profit.'

'I don't feel entirely comfortable with the idea of selling my book. As a reader, I don't mind buying books from authors but as an author I didn't relish selling to a reader. Odd, that.'

'But that's what you just did to us,' said Mike. 'You told us all about it, and it sounded good. If there had been a button to press, I might have bought it. That's all you have to do.'

WHY TAKE THE RISK?

Since losing my contract with the *Sunday Times*, I had trained in improvisation with Keith Johnstone, and now I teach impro myself. I'd been coached by Fenella Rouse, then Daniel Dresner, and I'd trained extensively to coach other people. I'd had books published in several languages. I did a lot of public speaking. I liked this new work, I was good at it, and I no longer depended on journalism for my income.

Lucky me.

So why risk the public humiliation of crowd-funding a novel – a historical novel, a book that absolutely nobody who had read my other books could possibly expect from me?

Because I wanted to, even though it scared me.

Because for years I had gone around with Queen Anne in my head, and Lady Masham and Mary and Bolingbroke and Oxford and Swift and Pope and Defoe. Because I'd put in so many hours of work already. Because I love making up stories, and the story I'd created was nothing if it wasn't told.

But how to get it out there? I was no salesman. Sure, I'd pitched ideas to magazine editors, sometimes ideas that turned into stories worth thousands of pounds, but pitching on the phone, in private, was by no means as high-stakes as public fundraising, which by definition needs to be noisy and highly visible.

What would Defoe have done? Or Swift? Or Pope?

I had little idea. At university, I'd devoted a lot of attention to their writing – the way they put words together – but little attention was given to how they made a living from it.

MAKE AN IMPACT QUICKLY

Mike had told me about Unbound, a publishing company established by authors for authors to crowd-fund their books.

I went to see them. Amazingly, they agreed to take me on. They hadn't read the book, mind you, but they liked the sound of it.

We made a film, in a graveyard, to promote the book on their website. And we talked strategy. How to draw in a variety of audiences: people who'd liked my previous (very different) books, people I've worked with, people who follow me on social media, people who don't know anything about me but love Queen Anne, or historical novels, or improvisation.

'Think of the kinds of offers you can make to each of those groups,' I was told. 'Some will only want to buy a copy of the book itself, but others might pay a lot of money for something more.'

'They key thing is to make a big impact quickly. If people see that lots of others have bought into your book, they'll want to be part of it too. If if looks like you're struggling to interest anyone, they might stay away.'

I drew up a list of things to offer would-be subscribers, ranging from £10 for an ebook to £1000 for a day of improvisation.

It soon became clear that the only way to bring people to the web page where they could buy these things was to create interesting content.

But how was I supposed to know what might interest other people? I remembered that workshop with Keith, improvising solo before an audience that had full permission to leave as soon as they lost interest. Was that what crowd-funding would be like?

I drew up some more lists: ideas for blog posts, things to put out on social media, films to catch people's attention.

WHAT COMES NEXT?

The stage goes dark.

Yes, what comes next?

Stirring music settles the audience. Spotlights circle rapidly. They halt eventually on a tiny, delicate young man at the front of the stage, wearing a wig and a frock coat, and supporting himself with a cane in each hand.

'Hello,' he says. 'You might think that crowd-funding is a new idea. But it is not. I invented it three hundred years ago – by accident. I did not set out deliberately to improve the prospects for writers everywhere. And I did not imagine that it would make me rich. Those were just happy by-products. I invented crowd-funding because I needed it. I loved to read – and I could not afford to buy books. I was in my mid twenties, with terrible prospects. As a child, I had been struck by tuberculosis of the spine, giving me back pain, fever, night sweats and difficulty standing. My vertebrae collapsed, giving me a stoop and making me shorter than everybody except for young children.

'On top of that, I was a Roman Catholic, in a country that had recently kicked out its King for being a Catholic. We were seen as dangerous agents of Rome, always plotting revolution. We were forbidden to live in central London, or to take a career in the army or navy. Not that I minded that very much – but Roman Catholics weren't allowed to go to university either, and that felt so unfair. Reading was what I was good at.

'But like I said, I could not afford to buy books. And I did not want to depend on my parents any longer. So I had to do something. But what? My talent was writing, and writers made no money. The people who made money were the printers, who were booksellers too. They held all the power. They would pay a tiny sum to authors for a book, and no matter how well it sold, in successive editions, that was all the writer received. Just look at Milton! Milton contracted to write *Paradise Lost*, the greatest long poem in the English language, for just twenty pounds. And out of that he only ever received five pounds.

'But I didn't allow this to put me off. I dedicated myself to getting my work out there, and some people were kind about it. (Others weren't.) Then I was lucky. I had a hit. My poem, "The Rape of The Lock", was a kind of parody of *Paradise Lost*, based around the true story of a man who stole a lock of hair, as a keepsake, from the woman it was attached to. That poem made a lot of money for my printer.

'And that is when I came up with my big idea. I told him I would write a translation of Homer's *Iliad* – my absolute favourite book, ever since I was a boy.

'He liked the idea. I said, "I'll do it in six instalments. And for each instalment you will pay me two-hundred guineas" – a lot of money at that time.

'He agreed.

'"Plus, I get seven hundred and fifty copies of the book for myself. Really beautiful copies, designed by me."

'"Od's blood," he said (that was an oath we used back then), "but all right. You are worth it."

'So this was my idea: to sell those seven hundred and fifty copies in advance, at two guineas each, to build a readership for the book before it was even printed, and fund the writing of the next one.

'I would no longer depend on publishers.

'The greatest writer alive, Joseph Addison, gave me the confidence to start. "Dear Pope," he wrote, "you must do it. Nobody else but you could do this."

'I could not believe it: Addison saying that to me!

'I had become friends with Addison by hanging around at Buttons, the fashionable coffee house where he held court with the other Whig wits. But I got sick of their teasing – I am Roman Catholic, so they always assumed that I was a Tory and a Jacobite. Were they right? I am not telling.

'I made other friends. The best of them was dear Jonathan Swift – a clergyman, but funny. He wrote a bit of satire on the side. Another great friend was the Queen's physician, Dr John Arbuthnot, who had his own rooms at court. Sometimes the great ministers of state joined us, like the Earl of Oxford – who would be called Prime Minister today, but we didn't use that title then – and his Tory coalition partner, Viscount Bolingbroke. These were my dearest friends.

'After I had announced my scheme, Swift promised to raise funds for me. "I'll get you a thousand guineas," he said. I could not believe it. We were in the Queen's own antechamber at the time. Swift knows a lot of important people! And he was true to his word. I owe so much to my dear friend Swift.

'With all this encouragement and support, I put an ad for my Homer in the third edition of "The Rape of the Lock". I promised that the first volume would be published exactly a year later.

'But I soon discovered that I had been rather optimistic. Which was humiliating. You see, subscribers do not just fall from heaven. They have to be found. The audience must be created. And I was not creating it fast enough. So ten weeks after the launch I was writing to all my friends, assuring them, not very convincingly, that failure would not be entirely mortifying.

'I had planned to publish a list of subscribers. It would be so impressive that everybody else would rush to join it. But it had to wait. For a year, nearly all my letter writing testified to the intense work of subscription. I had nightmares about journeys that never end, and not knowing which way to turn.

'How could I get people to pay?'

THE FUNDING TIMELINE

On the day I launched my crowd-funding campaign with Unbound, subscribers pledged £656 pounds. Amazing! The following day brought in another £900. Already I'd raised twelve per cent of the £11,241 I needed to pay for copy-editing, proof-reading, cover design, typesetting, conversion of the manuscript to an ebook, staffing and other overheads at Unbound, printing and distribution.

After a month, I had raised thirty-seven per cent.

After three months, fifty-three per cent.

After seven months, sixty-one per cent.

Oh, God.

What baffled me was why some people did pledge, and others didn't. The opportunity to name a character in the novel sold out immediately. But for weeks on end, nobody wanted to have their face appear as one of the characters.

The fundraising was hard work and, depending on how well I had slept, I could be enthusiastic and determined or utterly demoralised. I mentioned my struggle to my parents, and a day later I discovered that they had pledged for the book again, overnight.

HELLO, INNER CRITIC

What comes next?

No. Not that game any more. I can't bear it. I give up. I'm no good. I've failed.

Again and again I fell prey to the nagging self-critical voice in my head that told me I was failing.

Not long ago, under this kind of assault, I might have given up – just as I had put away the book, years ago, after a couple of rejections from publishers. But I didn't want to be put off so easily this time.

I wrote down some of the things that nagged at me, and I discovered that my inner critic sounded like a crazy distortion of a journalist, sneering at me that my happy experiments in writing historical fiction, and coaching, and improvisation were foolish and pathetic.

I could have tried to ignore this, but I didn't want to. Keith Johnstone, talking about how to create drama, had taught me a useful distinction between victims and heroes.

'A victim is a man in a hole,' he liked to say. 'And a hero is a man in a hole who is trying to get out.'

I wanted to be less of a victim, so I contacted lots of eminent and successful journalist friends and told them exactly what my inner critic had been saying, and sent them a link to my book. (Before sending the message, I had to take several deep breaths.) I didn't wait long for their replies, which were uniformly encouraging, funny, and sometimes also included a commitment to buy a copy of the book.

My inner critic could fuck off. From now on, I would devote less attention to the negative voices, and more to the ones that inspired me.

I wrote to Gyles Brandreth, explaining the book and asking if I could use his face as Defoe or Oxford.

He wrote back at once. *This sounds extraordinary, and exciting,* he replied. *We don't want to put off your potential public, so tread carefully with the faces you use! I'd be honoured to be either Defoe or the Earl of Oxford – I feel proper (aspirational) affinities to both. Keep me posted with developments.*

MY FRIENDS WERE INVALUABLE

'Eventually, I realised that I could not make anybody do anything. The key to getting subscribers was my friends. Jervas – bless him! – would be painting somebody's portrait and he would say, "You absolutely have to buy a copy of Pope's Homer. It's going to be amazing. Pope is so talented," he would say, "and all the best people are subscribing." As a result, some people would buy several copies to give to friends. Congreve, Garth and Halifax did the same, and others too.

'To help them do this, I would sometimes read passages of my work-in-progress to them. They felt more involved if I asked for their advice. Sometimes Halifax suggested I might have another look at such and such a line. I soon realised that with Halifax I could tell him I had taken another look, and that was enough: listening again, to exactly the same words, he would announce himself pleased with the changes. Everybody was happy!

'But at other times, my friends' suggestions were invaluable. Parnell, who read Greek, was especially helpful. Not having been to university, I did not read Greek. I tried to make up for that by getting hold of as many translations as I could find, and worked hard to make my own best version from what they had done before me – but sometimes I needed help.

'I gained more confidence when Richard Steele recommended

my *Iliad* to readers of his journal, the *Tatler*. But Addison said nothing. And did nothing. I mean, he pledged two guineas for his own copy, but he said nothing about my work to anybody else. Worse than that, he told me that one of his friends – a university man – was working on another translation, aimed to come out at the same time as mine. I can't tell you how much this distressed me.

'Meanwhile, my enemies attacked me, publishing pamphlets mocking my project and me personally. They would say, "Pope is translating the *Book of Tom Thumb* out of the original nonsense into Greek." Making fun all at once of my size and my lack of formal education. That kind of thing really hurt. But I never let people see that. Not even my friends.

'Others went further, suggesting that my translation was going to be some kind of Jacobite propaganda. They wanted to scare off would-be subscribers – make them afraid to have their name printed inside such a work.

After months of this, I was exhausted. But I was making good progress with the translation, and gradually, thanks to my friends, the list of subscribers grew longer and more and more impressive. It always lifted me to receive notice of payment. Every two guineas helped.

'Towards the end of the year, Jervas came home from a trip around Europe. He had been on the Grand Tour with his patron, the Earl of Burlington, helping him to choose art for his collection. Jervas made sure I was invited to the homecoming dinner. It was a wonderful evening. I tried to entertain people with stories, and involve them in my efforts. And I won a number of new subscribers.

'Mind you, by then I had learned to stop worrying so much

about rejection. As dear Swift used to tell me, some people will never want to buy a translation of Homer. And that is fine. For all I know, they do not like Homer. Or poetry. Or they are just short of funds. Or they intend to make a payment but keep forgetting – that happens too. It does not really matter. It is (usually) not personal.

'By the end of the year, I realised I had done enough. I was especially pleased with my list of subscribers: a princess royal, seventeen dukes, three marquesses, forty-nine earls – and many more. To anybody thinking of publishing by subscription I say: Do it! And I say: Beat that! And most importantly I say: You cannot do it on your own, so ask for help.'

WHAT COMES NEXT?

Don't you get it yet? It doesn't matter what comes next.

It might be the death of the Queen. It might be the advent of the Pretender, or George of Hanover. It might be the betrayal of your patron. Another writer might steal your idea and publish before you. The British newspaper industry might collapse. You might hire a community centre and find that nobody turns up to improvise with you. Your crowd-funding efforts might fail.

You can't possibly be ready for everything. The unexpected, by definition, will always catch you out. You can't control everything. The only thing you can control is how you react.

MADE IT, FINALLY

Having raised my funds, I had to submit my manuscript. To the people at Unbound, I said: 'I've basically written it already'. So they gave me a deadline, and with two days to go I started typing.

I'd been thinking about this book for more than fifteen years, and in that last weekend I wrote ten thousand additional words. But these words weren't about the early 1700s. They were about how this particular book had come together. Ten thousand words putting my own uncertain, stumbling process to the fore. Allowing it to be seen for what it was: much the same as anybody else's struggle to make things right: Defoe's, Queen Anne's, the Pretender's.

The reader's. Yours.

What was surprising was how easy it was. I felt like I was landing a plane after a long flight: not struggling, but watching myself sitting in the cockpit as the plane flew itself. It felt incredibly easy.

But of course I didn't get it all right.

At Unbound, they said: What is this shit you have stuck in here?

They said: What the fuck!

Actually, they didn't say that. Only my inner critic thought they said that.

What they really said was very nice, thank you for asking. But they thought that, instead of weaving the ten thousand words throughout the book, as I had done, perhaps they could be brought together as a kind of endmatter – stripped out from the historical novel but still part of the same book.

As you see, I took their advice. I also cut a huge amount out of the ten thousand. I'm still not sure they were right. A large part of me wants to resist that advice, and scatter the ten thousand words through the main text as before. It's an unresolved problem. And I'm not going to resolve it. You will make up your own mind about it. You will see for yourself whether a), you like the idea of a historical novel that is also self-referential or b), you hate it or c), don't feel very strongly either way. Or d), you may not bother to read this endmatter at all (in which case, does this sentence even really exist?).

Before the book was printed, I decided to send a copy of the manuscript to some of my subscribers, so they could tell me what they liked, and what they might like even more – something you can't easily do with conventional publishing. I have used some of the encouraging comments at the front of the book, and many of the editorial suggestions to improve the book itself.

Is it perfect now? Of course not. Because this business of creation is a constant struggle, between wishing for The Thing to be finished, and just continuing to put stuff out there until suddenly you realise it's done. The stuff may not be right. You may want to change it. You may actually change it. You may take fifteen years to create it, or just a weekend. You may have to kill a man, wear borrowed clothes, learn French or German, move back to Ireland or bake sourdough bread. You may struggle on alone, as if your project were a treasonable secret, or you might ask friends for help. But one day, eventually, it will look as if it could never have been any other way.

And it's so good to have been surprised.

251

Acknowledgements

I've never collaborated with so many people, over such a long period, on one project. I am blessed to have had your witty, thoughtful suggestions, generosity and (in several cases) sheer bloody hard work. In roughly chronological order: Thanks to my father Ian Flintoff for generally being such a Shakespeare nut; and my brother Crispin for showing me the way, aged about four, with a 'Shakespeare' play of his own about William the Conqueror. To the brilliant academics who taught Shakespeare and His Influence at Bristol University. To the screenwriter and former Holland Parker Sebastian Foster, for helping me to find Anne as a subject. To Harriet Green for putting up with it all, for years and years. To Stephanie Cabot for trying to get the early version out of me, and the publishers who turned that version of the book down, because that gave me the chance to make it better later. To the many writers I plagiarised openly, stealthily and sometimes diffusely; including (but not only) Shakespeare, Jonathan Swift, Alexander Pope, Daniel Defoe, Thomas Sheridan, Lord Byron, Robert Louis Stevenson, Joseph Conrad, F Scott Fitzgerald, Anthony Powell and Alasdair Gray. To Fenella Rouse and Steve Chapman for spurring me on. To the improvisers I have named already, the others I trained with, and especially Jude Claybourne, who played Anne and other characters in an hour-long improvised show that reduced some people in the audience to tears. To the Also Festival for inviting us to do that show. To the brilliant team at Unbound, who work so hard because they believe in what they're doing, and the lovely subscribers named in the following pages; especially those who reviewed the manuscript and suggested some brilliant changes. (Any remaining mistakes are mine.) To Gus Moore for help in a crisis with the portrait collages, and to the following individuals who kindly donated their modern faces to the historical bodies: Roses Urquhart, Jude Claybourne, Gyles Brandreth, Anna Milashevich, Robert Peston, Philippa Perry, Crispin Flintoff, Pernille Sørensen, Robert Twigger, Bilal Hafeez, me aged about 4, Will Steele, Antony Quinn, Ouardane Jouannot, Richard Coles, Hazel Slavin, Jason Henderson, Andreas Kömmling, Daniel Dresner and Hermione Jones.

Supporters

Unbound is a new kind of publishing house. Our books are funded directly by readers. This was a very popular idea during the late eighteenth and early nineteenth centuries. Now we have revived it for the internet age. It allows authors to write the books they really want to write and readers to support the writing they would most like to see published.

The names listed below are of readers who have pledged their support and made this book happen. If you'd like to join them, visit: www.unbound.co.uk.

Helen Abraham
Michael Abrahams
Geoff Adams
Aidan for Angela – enjoy!
C Appleby
Lottie Armitage
Nicola Ashton
Kelly Austin
Ann Ballinger
Jason Ballinger
Anne Barclay
Amanda Barry-Hirst

Stephen Baxter

Tina Bernstein

Octavius Black

Claire Bodanis

Estie Boshoff

Daniel Bradley

Lucie Bright

Julie Broadfoot

Alison Brooke

Martin Brooke

Julia, David, Joseph, Reuben & Zachary Brown

Maggie Brown

Richard Brown

Zachary Brown

Curt Buckley

Joseph Burne

Rosie Canning, Doctoral Researcher

Nicola Carr

Vickiesha Chabra

Steve Chapman

Tom Chatfield

Dean Clifford

Tim Cole

Richard Cook

Chris Corbett

Connor Courtney

Dycella Cummings-Palmer
Trisha D'Hoker
Catherine Daly
Richard Darkin
Naomi Darlington
Catherine Davies
Harriet Fear Davies
Leonora Davies
Peter Davies
Andrea Davis
Susan Deakin
Sasha Delaney
Karen Dobres
Wendalynn Donnan
Jenny Doughty
Pat Downes
Daniel Drage
Emma Ewing
Hermione Eyre
Peter Faulkner
Charlotte Featherstone
Crispin Flintoff
Ian and Deirdre Flintoff
David Foster
Ian Furbank
Jennifer Gallagher

Hilary Gallo
Mark Gamble
Alison Garner
Annabel Gaskell
Amro Gebreel
Stefan Geyer
Martha Gifford
Katie Glass
Chris Glynn
Lilian Goldberg
Caroline Goldthorpe
Chris Gostick
Gaylene Gould
Jenny Grant
Lucille Grant
Harriet Green
Suzette Green
Betsy Greer
Rohit Grover
Lisette Groves
Anna Guyer
Bilal Hafeez
Gretel Hallett
Katy Hamilton
Mishko Hansen
Kristen Harrison

Rachel Harrison
Matt Harvey
Sheila Hayman
Andrew Hearse
Alex Heffron
Tony Herr
Guy Hills
Grahame Hindes
Michael Horsley
Sophie Howarth
Richard Hsieh
Abigail Hunt
Sara Hunt
Vivien Hunt
Elaine Iley
Hermione Ireland
Johari Ismail
Brennan Jacoby
Ella Jakobson
Hilary Jeanes
Catherine Jennings
Leonie Jennings
Cat Jones
Hermione Jones
Kate Jones
Meghan Jones

Christina Kennedy

Dan Kieran

Simon Kingston

Doreen Knight

Hugh Knowles

Michaela Knowles

Roman Krznaric

Sascha Ladenius

Victoria Lambert

Lis Lambertsen

Muriel Lauvige

Kate Leask

Michelle Leer

Chrissy Levett

Beth Lewis

Eva Lindsay

Julia Lockheart

Joanne Ludlow

Jane Lunnon

Una Lynch

Andrea Mackay

Catherine Makin

Jane Marland

Ita Marquess

Iain Marrs

Carolyn Martin

Johnny Martin
Sandra McDonald
Kakia Michou
Anna Milashevich
Eila Millar
Gillian Miswardi
John Mitchinson
Kris Moore
Karin Mueller
Carlo Navato
David Nolan
Francis Norton
Laurence O'Bryan
Kevin O'Connor
Sara O'Connor
Lauren O'Farrell
Jenny O'Gorman
Julie Oldale
Alan Oldfield
Kate Onyett
Allison Ouvry
Lizzie Palmer
Joost Perreijn
Cynda Pierce
Justin Pollard
AM Poppy

Robert Poynton
Antony Quinn
Jack Rebaldi
Helen Reid
Jose Rey
Lyla Reynolds
Ellen Richardson
Kylie Rixon & Bill Harper
Debby Roberts
Robyn Roscoe
Andy Ross
Lynne Salisbury
Larissa Sanchez
Ian Sansom
Clare Savage
Chris Sayers
Danny Scheinmann
Caroline Schmitz
Kay Scorah
Carol Scott
Georgina Sears
Rebecca Sickinger
Yvonne Siegel
Adam Signy
Jacqui Sjenitzer
Hazel Slavin

Henriette B. Stavis

Mark Stevenson

Philip Stewart

Rachel Stirling

Annie Stogdale

Alan Terry

Catherine Thanki

John Thornton

Jenifer Toksvig

Rob Twigger

Elizabeth Van Pelt

Mark Vent

Charles Vollum

Jody Walker

David Waters

Fiona Watson

Laura Watts

Amanda Weston

Jane Wheeler

Lindsay Whitehurst

Janet Wilkinson

Rosie Willescroft

Jeremy Williams

James Wilson

Keeley Wilson

Mary Elisabeth Wingfield

Ralph Wirski
Gretchen Woelfle
Anne Wolff
Amelia Wray
Charles Wright
Rachel Wright
KyungSook Yang
Linda Youdelis
Mary Young
Vanessa Zainzinger